Dani Collins

THE CONSEQUENCE HE MUST CLAIM

HARLEQUIN PRESENTS®

Recycling programs
for this product may
not exist in your area.

ISBN-13: 978-0-373-13888-3

The Consequence He Must Claim

First North American Publication 2016

Copyright © 2016 by Dani Collins

HARLEQUIN®
www.Harlequin.com

Printed in U.S.A.

"Of all the memories I've lost, the most maddening is not remembering what it's like to make love to you."

Cesar bent and covered Sorcha's lips with his own, hard, but not hurtful. Seeming to catch himself at the last second and decide whether he wanted to plunder or merely sample.

Maybe he was waiting for a rush of memory, trying to remember how their first kisses had tasted and felt. She remembered. She wanted to protest and turn away from his kiss, but her body knew him in a primal way that made her whole being soften in welcome. Her hand lifted to caress the stubble on his cheek, urging him to linger, playing her mouth against his in invitation.

With a gruff sound deep in his throat, he took control of the kiss. He claimed in a way that felt familiar, yet new. He stole, but gave back at the same time, started to pull away, then returned as if he couldn't help himself. The teasing sent flutters of arousal through her, burning her blood to the ends of her limbs, making her fingers and toes tingle.

The Wrong Heirs

Securing the billionaires' legacies!

Meet Alessandro Ferrante, Italian tycoon, and
Cesar Montero y Rosales, Spanish aristocrat.

Their whole lives, they have done their duty,
and commanded everything in their sight.

But after a mix-up at the hospital, they're left
holding the *wrong* baby, and their lives are turned
upside down in a heartbeat!

With their heirs back in their rightful place
and their legacies ensured, the only thing left
to secure are their brides!

Don't miss

The Marriage He Must Keep

January 2016

and

The Consequence He Must Claim

February 2016

The powerful new duet
from Harlequin Presents author Dani Collins!

Canadian **Dani Collins** knew in high school that she wanted to write romance for a living. Twenty-five years later, after marrying her high school sweetheart, having two kids with him, working several generic office jobs and submitting countless manuscripts, she got "The Call." Her first Harlequin Presents romance novel won the Reviewers' Choice Best Book Award for Best First in Series from *RT Book Reviews*. She now works in her own office, writing romance.

Books by Dani Collins

Harlequin Presents

Vows of Revenge
Seduced into the Greek's World
The Russian's Acquisition
An Heir to Bind Them
A Debt Paid in Passion
More than a Convenient Marriage?
No Longer Forbidden?

Seven Sexy Sins

The Sheikh's Sinful Seduction

The 21st Century Gentleman's Club

The Ultimate Seduction

One Night With Consequences

Proof of their Sin

Visit the Author Profile page
at Harlequin.com for more titles.

This story is for Doug, Cesar to my Sorcha.
I love you.

PROLOGUE

Eight months ago...

SORCHA KELLY ENTERED the hospital with determined steps. It was coming up to three weeks. They *had* to let her see him. Especially now that she knew. Not just suspected but *knew* she was pregnant.

Before this, Cesar Montero's family had only seen her as his personal assistant. Devoted, absolutely. His entire family appreciated her dedication. They couldn't have transitioned the running of the multinational engineering firm back into his father's capable hands without her. She'd been invaluable in those first difficult days after the crash.

But she was only his PA and he'd been unconscious, with visitors limited to his immediate family. Plus his fiancée, of course.

How, exactly, did an unconscious man get engaged? That's what Sorcha wanted to know.

Aside from crossing paths at a few family events, Cesar hadn't even been seeing Diega. The agreement between the families to eventually merge assets via marriage had been an expectation, not a written contract or even an emotional one.

Cesar's mother was the one who'd been pressing to formalize the engagement. Cesar had confided his reluctance to follow through with it to Sorcha that last day.

Obviously his family didn't know Cesar had left Sorcha the evening of the crash to inform Diega the marriage wouldn't happen. He'd seen Diega. The woman had admitted to authorities that he'd been at her house and left again, so why was Diega acting like the marriage was on? Like plans had advanced from "maybe" to "absolutely"?

How had she gone from family friend to fiancée in the sliver of time that Cesar had spent at the bottom of a cliff in a bashed-up car?

The question tortured Sorcha every moment of every day while she waited for Cesar to wake up and explain himself.

He'd stayed in a coma for so long, however, she'd begun to anticipate that if she did turn up pregnant, this baby might be a comfort to his family. Then he had awoken and she knew he would explain that *she* was meant to be at his side, not Diega.

Except that didn't happen. His father had dropped by the office to explain that Cesar had lost a week's worth of memories prior to the crash. He didn't recall the ribbon cutting on the bridge in Madrid and was quite anxious to oversee it, *el Excelentísimo,* Señor Montero had added with one of his distracted frowns, the one that suggested he was exasperated by humans and their mortal frailties.

Sorcha had stared, speechless, at the Duke of Castellon. Cesar's private celebration of the bridge with her once they'd returned to Valencia had given way to a heart-to-heart and eventually their life-changing body-to-body connection. Cesar remembered *nothing* of that?

How did one process such news? All she'd felt was a void inside her. Like their magical afternoon hadn't happened.

Somehow she had swallowed back a dry lump and asked if she could see him. "Not necessary," his father had told her.

It really was. Sorcha wouldn't believe Cesar's loss of memory until he'd told her himself, especially now that the evidence of their lovemaking was confirmed by a tiny pink stripe on a wand.

Surely if he saw her, he would remember?

As the doors of the private hospital slid closed behind her, her mouth was arid, her skin numb, her limbs electrified by three weeks of sustained tension. Rough treatment in her teens had taught her how to keep a mask of confident indifference on her face, however. And working with Cesar had granted her certain entitlements these past three years. She approached the doors to the interior as though she had every right to enter.

"Señorita?" a clerk at the lobby desk called, halting her as efficiently as the electronically sealed doors. She wore a smart, modern uniform and was well foiled by the clean, peach and plum tones of the lobby.

"Bon dia," Sorcha said, using Valencian, which she had learned from Cesar, rather than her excellent Spanish, which might label her an outsider. She added a respectful "Sister," then said. "Sorcha Kelly for Cesar Montero," punctuated with her I-screen-visitors-too smile. *We're practically twins.*

The Sister tapped keys on her computer, then smiled benignly. "I don't have your name on the list."

"I'm sure if you call, he'll confirm he wants to see me," Sorcha assured her.

As the Sister picked up her phone to dial, the entrance doors swished open and Diega Fuentes entered. Diega Fuentes y Losa de Mateu, to be precise, daughter of the Marques de los Jardines de Las Salinas. She definitely looked rich enough to have more names than she could use. Her tall, slender silhouette was practically haloed in designer labels with imaginary arrows pointing to her purse and earrings, lipstick and strappy heels. Her sundress was a fluttery cornflower blue with white polka dots, her sleek black hair a stunning frame for her elegant bone structure, lightly golden skin and bottomless eyes.

Sorcha hadn't been able to fully cover the dark circles under her eyes and wore her work clothes—a gray pencil skirt with a matching vest over a white top. Given the worry she'd been enduring, along with a hint of morning sickness, her complexion was probably greener than her eyes.

Cesar's "fiancée" did a small double take, then sauntered toward Sorcha.

Sorcha hated her. Not because she was claiming to be engaged to Cesar, but because everything about her struck Sorcha as fake and calculating. Sorcha knew how to keep her feelings to herself, however, so she worked up the warm smile she'd perfected for Cesar's many, *many* conquests.

And she wouldn't even think of *those* women right now. She was not one of a crowd. She wasn't.

Ignoring the weight of insecurity that descended on her, she moved forward to meet Diega. "Señorita Fuentes. Thank goodness. I'll go up with you to see Cesar."

"Did he call you?" Diega asked with mild surprise and what might have been a flicker of uneasiness in her lashes.

Sorcha was nothing if not honest, but she wasn't above small prevarications when the stakes were this high. "His father said he was anxious to catch up on work, so..." *Obviously he needs me*, she intimated.

Diega took a small breath and manufactured a tight smile, like she was preparing for a difficult conversation. Sliding her gaze to the Sister, she asked, "May we speak privately...? Perfect," she murmured as they were pointed to a small lounge off the lobby.

The room was bright, but looked onto the street. Eggplant-colored cushioned benches lined the walls and a television on low volume hung in the corner. The space was no doubt utilized by drivers and other personnel who were required to wait for their employers, people not exalted enough to ascend to the patients' rooms.

Sorcha choked back a feeling of lowered circumstances that hadn't sat so jagged and bitter in the back of her throat since her father's death had drastically changed her mother's situation in their Irish village.

Controlling a wave of panic, Sorcha conjured an expression of mild interest while Diega took great care closing the door, trapping them in the fishbowl.

"You understand that he's lost a piece of his memory," Diega said in what Sorcha imagined was supposed to be a break-it-to-her-gently tone.

"I've worked with him for almost three years. He hasn't forgotten that, has he?"

"No, of course not," Diega said smoothly. "But he's not up to working. His doctor suggests he put that off for a few months. If you have a concern at the office, you should take it up with Javiero."

Diega didn't stoop to titles. She was on a first-name basis with Cesar's father, as her casual tone demonstrated. Even when the titles were the highest in the land.

Sorcha swallowed. "He's more than my employer. When you work that closely with someone, you care about his well-being. I'd like him to know we're all wishing him well."

If her firm tone said, "Shut up and let me through the doors," she couldn't help it. Three weeks without Cesar's distantly amused mouth, framed by sculpted stubble, was an eternity. Three weeks without aqua eyes that always met hers, never strayed below her collar, yet still conveyed masculine admiration, had left her dying of thirst.

"Sorcha." Diega lowered to perch on the edge of a bench.

Oh, how grotesquely patronizing she was as she nodded at a spot opposite.

Sorcha bit back what she wanted to say—*don't call me that*. If she had to say "Señorita Fuentes," she expected to be called Ms. Kelly in return. "I'd rather stand," Sorcha said.

Diega lowered her gaze, suggesting an ability to hold on to her dignity even when faced with impertinence.

Forcing down the sort of curse that never crossed her lips, Sorcha set her bottom on the corner of a cushion. "Yes?" she prompted Diega.

"I understand why you feel so concerned. Why you think there's some sort of familiarity between you." Her dark eyes came up and they were tar-like, sucking Sorcha forward into suffocating blackness. "He felt very guilty when he came to see me that night."

Don't betray a thing, her gut told her, but she licked her lips and asked, "Did he?" in a raspy whisper.

Cesar might not have been in love with Diega, but he was a man of honor. "I shouldn't be doing this," he'd said, right before they'd gone past the point of no return. He'd left her while she slept, leaving a text on her phone. Gone to see Diega.

It had stung to wake alone, but after everything they'd talked about leading up to falling into bed—or rather, falling onto his office sofa—

Sorcha had been convinced he'd left to cut things off with Diega. Surely that's what he had done. Surely.

But then, here was Diega claiming they were engaged...

"I haven't wanted to bring this up. *With any-one*," Diega said firmly. "What is the use in smudging reputations or pointing fingers when faced with much more serious concerns? Especially when he assured me that he was simply sowing his final oats." Her lip curled in a reflection of distaste.

"What?" That's what he had called her? *Oats?*

The persistent ache in Sorcha's chest, the one that had been seeded by his leaving her and going to Diega in the first place, expanded with a creeping burn. "That wasn't—"

"You needn't deny it," Diega said with a muted smile. "I appreciate your trying to spare my feelings."

Did Diega *have* feelings? As far as Sorcha could see, Diega's ego had caught a brush of dust. Only mild annoyance tainted her expression. No genuine hurt.

Nevertheless, she gave a little nod of determination that Sorcha read as being seen as an unwelcome bug in the house. Something to be squashed and swept out.

"I had hoped we could both be spared this

conversation, but… He said you were planning to resign when we marry. That's right, isn't it?"

Sorcha searched Diega's dark eyes, trying to find the trick because she was sure there was one in the question.

"You told him you don't care for me," Diega explained, her smile now philosophical. "I'm sorry you feel that way."

"I didn't say it like that," Sorcha blurted. It struck her as bizarre that, for some reason, she found herself trying to cushion the impact to Diega's feelings, trying to salvage a relationship she didn't care about, but it was ingrained in her not to upset the women in Cesar's life.

She was glad she was sitting because she felt very off balance. She had told Cesar that it was one thing to field calls from last night's airline hostess or a model he took on vacation. It was something entirely different to stand between a wife and her husband. A potential fiancée in this case, but she'd seen the writing on the wall. Diega was gracious and elegant, but completely unafraid to pull rank.

While Sorcha had grown fond of being the most important woman in Cesar's life.

He had told Diega she had said she didn't like her? That was really unnerving.

"However you said it, once he realized you would be leaving, he did what he does. Didn't he?" Diega said with a condescending tuck of her chin.

"What do you mean?" Sorcha asked, but one glance at Diega's pitying smile told her exactly what she meant. "It wasn't like that," Sorcha muttered, heart skidding through its own roadside barrier to plummet down an embankment. She had meant more to him than a notch on his bedpost, hadn't she? She was an honest person, especially with herself. She hadn't been delusional about his feelings toward her.

Had she?

But had she really thought they were going to marry and live happily ever after? Their lovemaking had been impetuous, but somewhat inevitable. She had given in to yearnings that had gripped her from the first. But had she really imagined it was the beginning of something serious? Of a life with him?

Deep in her heart of hearts, she knew she wasn't the kind of woman a man like Cesar married. Facing that made her squirm inwardly, putting her right back in that mind-set of being small and worthless again.

She had thought they were friends, though! That he really cared for her.

"You're legendary among his inner circle, you know," Diega said. "The PA who held out and therefore held her job for three whole years." Like that was a joke.

It was a deep mark of pride for her, but Sorcha found herself tightening her lips, not mollified in the least that gossip abounded about her even when there was no shame attached to how she was conducting herself. She *hated* being talked about.

"To be honest, I would have trusted you after we were married," Diega said with a lofty elevation of her head. "You could have had a successful career for years to come. But of course we can't go backward now. I'm very sorry it's come to this."

Liar, Sorcha thought. Then, in a panic, wondered, *Come to what?*

"He was very remorseful. Sorry he'd done it when we were so close to announcing things. Sorry, I think, that he'd made you into a conquest when he had had so much respect for you before."

His respect was gone? Sorcha's heart stopped, ears ringing so loudly, she barely heard the rest of what Diega was saying. She had a terrible feeling her mouth was hanging open. She was really nauseous now. Bile burned the back of her throat.

"His ego got the best of him, Sorcha. You know what he's like. You were the one that looked about to get away. It's, well, it's sad, isn't it?" She cocked her head. They were friends, discussing the pitiful behavior of an incorrigible rake. "He promised he would be faithful once we were engaged and married, but he wanted me to know because you'd still be working for him."

"I don't intend to cheat on her," Cesar had said that day in his office, referring to Diega. Had he viewed Sorcha as his last chance to enjoy his freedom?

"He wanted to come clean because you work for him," Diega continued. "You're not one of his passing fancies. He rightly felt he had to tell me and I admit I wasn't prepared to start our engagement with you still in the picture. I insisted he end your employment as soon as possible, not keep you on until we married. I'll have to live with the fact that I sent him away rather than letting him stay to talk things out. If he hadn't been in such a rush to secure our engagement, he wouldn't have been on the road that evening, trying to avoid that stalled truck…"

Sorcha shook her head. No. That was not what had happened. "He and I talked that day," she said, not willing to accept this without a fight, but she stopped herself. Cesar's confidences were exactly that. She never, ever repeated the things he told her.

"About his doubts? He was a bachelor with cold feet who wanted to persuade you to sleep with him! I wouldn't give much weight to any-thing he said under those circumstances."

Cold feet, yes, he'd definitely been suffering that, but there were other things. "The way you talk about your family. Our family is a business. I prefer it, but I sometimes wonder what it would be like to be close like that," he'd said pensively.

His family's negotiation to merge with the Fuentes family was very big business. Those sorts of deals weren't dropped willy-nilly just so a man could sleep with his secretary, she knew that, but...

But he had asked her to stay.

"The kindest thing you could do," Diega said, like she was offering step-by-step instructions on how a mistress should conduct herself after dis-covery by a wife, "would be to leave. I'll speak to Javiero, ensure you're written the best possi-ble reference. Given Cesar's condition, none of us wants a scandal. He's facing a long, difficult recovery as it is. You don't want to set him back, do you? I believe you do care for him."

I'm pregnant, Sorcha thought as waves of hot and cold humiliation washed over her.

Was she really just the one that almost got away? She couldn't believe it. He'd seemed so *real* that day. Not the playboy Diega was refer-ring to, but the man capable of reflecting on his life and deciding who and what he really was.

"He doesn't even remember it, Sorcha," Diega said with soft compassion. "I'm grateful. I plan to forget it as completely as he has. And we will marry," she added, as if making a resolution that would be engraved into platinum. "We all know what sort of life he leads and what sort of wife he needs."

Sorcha stopped breathing, recalling that she had confided some of her background to Cesar that day. Had he mentioned any of that to Diega during their little heart-to-heart?

"I won't claim he doesn't value your work, but I hope you weren't thinking he was in love with you?"

Sorcha looked at her nails, manicure neglected in these past stressful weeks, cuticles chewed with anxiety.

I'm pregnant, she thought again, but she could just imagine how that would play out: Cesar denying it was even possible, his parents thinking it was a ploy on her part to take advantage of his riches. Paternity tests. Delving into her background to discredit her.

She couldn't do that to her mother.

Revealing her pregnancy would create bitterness all around and even if she could prove she was telling the truth, then what? Did she think he would marry her? Claim his child?

At best she might see a settlement, but she and

her sisters were evidence that even when rich men made babies and appeared to love them, they didn't always make provisions for them. That was the real source of her shame over her upbringing—that her father had left them with no indication they were as important to him as he'd led them to believe while he was alive. All the denigration in the village combined didn't equal the rejection she'd felt when it became obvious her father had left them nothing.

Not even the ability to hold up their heads.

Her mother had maintained that he'd loved them, which had kept her going, but Sorcha didn't even have such a declaration of love from Cesar.

He could very well have been using her. Ticking a final box.

Did she really want to put herself through all of that for a check in the mail once a month that would just make her feel like a whore? Her mother had managed without support payments and Sorcha would rather spare herself the humiliation of begging for scraps.

"You were planning to resign," Diega said *again*. "Do. Before his father has to hear about this." *Because I'll tell him*, she seemed to threaten.

Sorcha's eyes burned. "I want to see him," she said in a thin voice.

"Please, Sorcha. I've been far more civil than anyone could expect me to be. Show me you have enough remorse, enough *class*, not to make this worse."

Class. Ouch. Perhaps Diega did know where she came from.

I hate you, Sorcha asserted silently as she rose and leveled her chin. Beyond the windows, the sunny brilliance of Valencia was a streaked image of blue sky and concrete gray, chrome and luxury-car black, early summer flowers blooming in a kaleidoscope of colors between.

"He has my number," she said.

A tiny snort sounded, letting Sorcha know Cesar wouldn't be dialing it on Diega's watch. Then she veiled her triumph with good manners, standing and opening the door.

Sorcha didn't offer her hand, didn't look for Diega's. She was convinced Cesar would reach out to her, though. He had to. She wouldn't disgrace herself the way her mother had, pleading for favors from the family of her children's father only to be cast out anyway. If Cesar didn't remember how and why they'd wound up making love, he'd think she was exactly as Diega painted her: one more woman who'd fallen under his spell.

No, if he called her, she wanted it to be because he missed her. It would be better that way, she assured herself. She wouldn't be accused of trying to trap him with a baby. She'd know it was about her, not duty or obligation.

In the short term, however, that left her with one option: go home to tell her mother she'd made the same mistake she'd grown up with.

CHAPTER ONE

Present day...

SORCHA ENDED THE call and grabbed a tissue to let the tears release. Oh, she was homesick and filled with self-pity, not that she had wanted her mum to hear it.

Mum was probably doing the same thing. They were both pretending Sorcha's situation wasn't a disaster and this emergency caesarian in London was the icing on the cake. Things really couldn't get any worse.

She *so* wished she'd managed to get home before going into labor. She might have found a decent job here after quitting right after that disastrous talk with Diega, but Ireland was where her heart was. If her son wouldn't be recognized as Spanish, like his father, she had at least wanted him born on Irish soil.

It hadn't happened.

Her nurse, Hannah, came in with a wheelchair

and a chipper offer to take her down to meet him. Finally.

That brought a smile to Sorcha's face. She might be lonely here, but at least she had her son now. She would only be in hospital a few days, Hannah assured her, while the staff confirmed they were both healthy enough to be released. Then Sorcha could make the trek on the ferry and soon be surrounded by the people who loved her.

Her family would adore her son. Little things like being illegitimate just made him more like the rest of them.

Hannah asked how she was feeling and Sorcha started to explain that she had had every intention of delivering naturally, but had gone into labor early and the cord had been in the way, so they'd had to send her for emergency surgery. It had been quite dramatic, arriving on the heels of a tourist bus crash and at the same time as another woman needing an emergency caesarian section in the theater next to hers.

She broke off as they entered the nursery to find crying babies and the other mum from last night. Not that she'd met the stunning Italian woman. Sorcha had only caught a glimpse of a man she'd thought must have been the woman's husband. She'd heard him speaking Italian on the phone as she was wheeled past him.

"Hello. I heard we were competing for the surgeon's attention last night," she greeted. "I'm Sorcha Kelly."

Wait a minute. That wasn't the man from last night. He looked sharper, despite his stubble of beard growth. His hair was decidedly shorter.

He offered a polite nod. "Alessandro Ferrante. My wife, Octavia, and our son, Lorenzo," he said, then glanced at his wife. "That is the name we agreed upon, is it not?"

The other woman seemed…shell-shocked. If she felt anything like Sorcha did, Sorcha sympathized. The anesthetic had made her sluggish and every movement caused the incision across her abdomen to whimper.

Octavia exchanged a look with her husband that Sorcha might have tried to decipher, but the nurse had fetched and loosely wrapped her baby. He was crying furiously, like he'd been at it awhile, making her very sorry he'd had to wait.

"Do you mind, Mr. Ferrante?" Hannah said, pirouetting a finger in the air.

He apologized and turned with the sort of male briskness that men showed when confronted with a woman's demand for modesty.

Sorcha couched a smile. He reminded her of Cesar. Not so much in looks, although they were both very dark and handsome, but in the way he emanated vitality and owned the room.

Cesar, she thought, and missed him all over again. She desperately wanted to be with her family when his wedding took place this weekend, not here in the hospital, nursing melancholy along with his baby.

Murmuring a tender greeting, she closed her arms around the delicious weight of the bundled infant. *Hers*, she thought. Not a Montero, just as she wasn't a Shelby. "Enrique," she added in a whisper. Cesar's middle name. She would call him Ricky—

Wait. Something wasn't right.

He was crying so earnestly the sound broke her heart. She instinctively wanted to do anything soothe him, but…

Distantly she heard Octavia say in a choked voice, "That's—"

"Octavia," her husband interrupted with an undertone of warning.

Sorcha wasn't really tracking the other people in the room. She cocked her head, perplexed, as she tried to figure out why her feelings for this baby were protective, but not maternal.

"Just put him to the breast. He'll latch. They know what to do," Hannah urged.

"I don't think—" Sorcha couldn't even voice her thoughts, they were so bizarre. She found her gaze lifting and looked across to the baby Octavia was trying to soothe. Octavia rubbed his back and rocked him and for some weird reason, that boy's cries went through Sorcha's skin like rippling waves, moving things in her she couldn't even name.

As Octavia held Sorcha's stare in a kind of eerie transfixion, she lowered the baby so Sorcha could see his face.

Sorcha looked at the squalling infant. His brows were wrinkled in a way that she knew, like an imprint on a part of her that recognized its own kind. That frown of displeasure was all Cesar, and those miniature lips—they were a replica of the mouth she'd seen in the mirror all her life.

Horror washed over her in a clammy rush.

"What's wrong?" Hannah asked as the other nurse blurted out something, but Sorcha wasn't listening.

"How did you…?" she began, sharp suspicion rising. She cut herself off. It was beyond outlandish. People didn't steal babies. They certainly didn't sit across from you and taunt you with it. That was something from a psycho thriller film.

But her heart was pounding in terror. Confusion and certainty warred and she began to shake under the strain of it.

Baring the ankle of the baby she held, she turned the tag with a trembling hand. It read, Kelly.

But this wasn't her baby. *That* was her baby. That woman held her baby.

Beginning to panic, Sorcha flashed her gaze to Octavia's, not sure what she expected. An evil grin?

Octavia's lower lip was trembling. "They wouldn't believe me," she said weakly.

"Believe what?" Hannah asked.

"My wife is confused," Alessandro said, and moved between Sorcha and her baby, trying to take the infant Octavia held.

"Don't," Sorcha blurted, and understood the kind of irrational yet powerful instinct that drove animals to overcome self-preservation, confront dangerous predators and protect their young with every last breath in their body. "Don't touch him."

The baby she held was screaming her ears off and part of her wanted to comfort him, but that was her baby over there. That one.

She struggled to her feet and came across to Octavia. The other woman had tears on her cheeks.

"No one would believe me," Octavia told her again. "I wanted to feed him, but he needs his own mama and they wouldn't give me mine…"

They clumsily exchanged babies and the dizzying panic that had nearly overwhelmed Sorcha began to subside. Her heart continued to race and adrenaline burned up her veins.

"I believe you," she said, smiling shakily now that her son's sweet scent filled her nostrils. She kissed his cheek and clasped him against her chest, knowing with unequivocal certainty that this was her son. Cesar's son. "Of course we know our own babies."

What the hell had just happened? *What the hell?*

As if reflecting the emotions Sorcha felt, Octavia nodded, eyes closing as she bent her head over the baby she obviously loved and had been aching to hold.

How long had she been sitting here holding Enrique, trying to convince them to give her the right baby? In the face of that torture, Octavia had still tried to soothe Sorcha's son.

A funny little bond formed between them even as Sorcha seated herself and brought Enrique to her breast. Silence descended as both boys finally received the meal they'd been begging for. Still very bewildered, Sorcha exchanged a teary smile with Octavia.

And became aware of profound silence.

"What are you *doing*?" Alessandro's gruff male voice was astounded.

"Can't you see they mixed them up? Look at him," Octavia said.

"It's impossible," Hannah said. "We have very strict protocols. They couldn't have been switched.

You shouldn't be doing this," she warned, rolling the tag around on Enrique's ankle. It read, Ferrante—Boy. "You both have it wrong."

Now that she was seated and had her baby calmed, Sorcha was shifting from disbelief to outrage. How could the hospital mess up something this important?

"*You* have it wrong," Sorcha said firmly, brushing Hannah's hand from her son. If she thought they were going to switch back, they had another think coming. She was ready to draw blood. Only the fact she was holding a fragile newborn kept her seated and rational. "Test them. You'll see we're right."

Chaos ensued as the nurses tried to convince the mothers they'd made a mistake. Thankfully Octavia was as adamant as Sorcha.

Finally the surgeon, Dr. Reynolds, arrived. She was taken aback and involved the hospital administration at once, all the while assuring them the chance of a mix-up was highly unlikely. She wanted to run DNA tests, and would do a blood test now. "It won't be conclusive, but it could certainly determine if a baby is *not* with the right pair of parents."

A jumble of activity left Sorcha feeling like a dupe in a three-card shuffle, trying to follow what they were doing and maintain some control over the situation. While a technician took a blood sample from the baby she held, no one seemed to make note that she knew—*knew*—that Cesar's blood type was A. She had worked for him for three years! She knew everything about him.

Eventually everyone cleared out, the men going to look at security tapes while one nurse stayed behind to give her and Octavia slings to snuggle the babies while they dozed in their rockers. Neither of them was prepared to release the infant they each held.

Sorcha tried to relax, chatted briefly with Octavia, but her mind kept tracking back to the fact she'd put Cesar's name on her admittance form. It had been an emergency delivery. Her mother was registered as next of kin, but Sorcha had wanted Cesar identified as the baby's father if the worst had happened.

They wouldn't contact him without speaking to her first, would they?

Cesar Montero subtly pinched the bridge of his nose, fighting a dull headache and a desire to tell his fiancée that he didn't give a flying rat's behind about who sat where at their wedding reception. Social arrangements were his mother's bailiwick. If he'd still had Sorcha, she would have handled this, freeing him up for more important things.

Actually, he'd bet any money she would challenge him with "What's more important than your wedding?" She'd always been quick to push a family-first agenda, teasing him for being a scientist wired for logic. She'd known when she could give him a nudge and when to back off, though, along with how to plow through minutiae so he didn't get bored and lose patience. Most important, she had been able to make decisions on her own.

But Sorcha was gone, damn her. Without any notice or explanation. She'd left while he'd still been in the hospital, barely awake from his coma. According to his father, she'd discussed it with Cesar in the week that was missing from his memory. Given that he'd been unconscious in those first weeks after the accident, and his father had his own assistant, he could imagine she had felt redundant, but she must have known he'd be back to work eventually. His father could have found her a temporary position in the organization or simply offered her paid leave. She'd had enough vacation time stockpiled.

Jumping ship was unacceptable. If his father hadn't already written her a glowing reference, Cesar would have been reluctant to. He could have used her more than ever in these first months back at work, as he first went into the office on crutches at his own chemical engineering plant, and had more recently begun resuming the takeover from his father on the rest of the family enterprise.

She was just an employee, he reminded himself, irritated that he was letting her absence rile him. Yes, he missed her efficiency, but he wasn't a sentimental man. Being friendly with a colleague wasn't the same as being friends. For all the times she'd been more blunt than he appreciated, their relationship had been a professional one. He directed, she delivered. Sulking because she hadn't played cards with him in the hospital was not something he would stoop to.

At least she had understood simple instructions, he thought as he glanced at the watch that had started pulsing on his wrist. Diega noticed and looked at him as if he'd kicked her Siamese cat. His mother caught on and tsked a noise of disappointment at his rudeness.

"I asked not to be interrupted," he informed both women, making sure his new assistant heard his displeased tone as he touched the face of his smart watch.

He automatically adjusted the volume in his earpiece as his assistant said, "They claim it's an emergency. It's a hospital in London."

His thoughts leaped to Sorcha, even though there was no reason to expect she would be ill or injured, but he had tracked her on social media far enough to know she was working in that city. Still, if she needed medical attention, she wouldn't list him as a contact. She had family in Ireland. She was off the company benefits, working for someone else.

He almost refused the call, unable to think of another reason a hospital in London would want to speak to him. He had a vague thought about his siblings' whereabouts, but neither his brother nor sister was in that city. Hell, he would wind up returning this call later if he didn't take it now and he would go out of his skull if he didn't accomplish something constructive with his morning.

"Un momento," he said, stepping away from the women. "Cesar Montero," he stated, accepting the call.

"Cesar Montero…y Rosales?" a female voice asked.

"Sí." He grew more alert at the use of his full name. "Who's calling?"

She identified herself as an official for the hospital. "Did Ms. Kelly tell you to expect my call?"

"No." He frowned as he absorbed this *was* about Sorcha.

"Oh." She sounded confused. "This is the information she gave on her admittance form. Am I speaking to the correct person? Will you confirm a few details for me?"

"Sí," he said and gave her his birth date and residential address as requested. He rubbed where the ache in his brow intensified. "What is this about?"

"You haven't spoken to Ms. Kelly today?" She sounded surprised. The silence that followed struck him as a retreat. She was cautious now.

Instinct made him say carefully, "I've been tied up. She left a message, but I haven't listened to it yet."

"But you're aware she was admitted last night?"

"Yes," he lied, while his heart jolted painfully. They'd asked if he'd spoken to her, he reminded himself. That meant she was speaking. "I've been anxious for news," he added. He was a scientist at heart, but he'd studied conversational manipulations at his mother's knee. "What can you report?"

"Well, it's difficult news, I'm afraid. There is a very small possibility the babies have been switched." She paused, allowing him to react.

He didn't have a reaction. A chasm of confusion opened in him, one he didn't want to betray to the woman on the phone, or the two women behind him. He could hear their silence as they waited for him to wrap up this annoying interruption.

"Obviously we'll be running a DNA test, but

we're hoping a blood test can offer some clarity. How soon could you get to a clinic? Our hospital will cover the charges, but we're anxious for the results."

Cesar choked out a laugh. "Are you…?"

He realized where he was. He jerked around to see both his fiancée and his mother staring at him. His mother waved an impatient hand at the seating plan spread across the dining room table. Diega's features sharpened with query.

The air grew too thick for his lungs. In a kind of daze, he held up a staying finger and walked through the French doors onto the small balcony, closing them behind him. With great care, he lowered the voice that had begun to elevate, looking below to ensure there were no listening ears in the courtyard. His gaze blindly scanned the familiar landscape of his youth: immaculate gardens left barren for winter, dormant grapevines across acres of vineyard, the distant sound of waves washing the shoreline of the Med.

"Are you telling me you want me to provide a sample for a paternity test?" he asked in disbelief.

"Please don't mistake me. We have no reason to doubt Sorcha Kelly's identification of you as the father. The issue is whether she is the mother of the baby she is currently nursing. As you can imagine, we're anxious to have this cleared up."

He couldn't speak. It took him a long moment to realize he wasn't thinking any thoughts. His mind was completely blank.

Was he still feeling the effects of the concussion? No. This was the sort of thing no one in the world could make sense of.

Finally he drew a long ragged breath. "I can clear up my side of things very quickly," he said, his voice flat and sharp. "I would remember if—" He cut himself off. Swore aloud as his condition struck him like a sledgehammer. *Again.*

There was no feeling like opening a door where a memory was stored and finding only an empty shelf. It was beyond frustrating. It was like being robbed and if there was one thing he hated above anything, it was a thief.

"Mr. Montero?" she prompted in his ear.

Maybe he didn't remember sleeping with his secretary, but it didn't mean he hadn't.

At least his damaged brain was still agile enough to deal logically with the present situation. The only way to determine if he'd fathered a child in the mysterious missing week was to provide a blood sample.

Of course, that flash of logic did nothing to alleviate the fact that his mind was exploding with questions. Sorcha had promised—sworn with as much solemnity as a bride taking her wedding vows—that she would never sleep with him.

He had believed her. It had taken a long time for him to trust her. He didn't give his trust easily, not since the industrial espionage that had nearly bankrupted his family. She knew enough about that to know he wouldn't tolerate lies of any sort.

But he had wanted to sleep with her.

So had she broken her promise and slept with him? Or would this test prove she had identified the wrong man as the father of her child? Perhaps she'd left Spain because she was pregnant and for some reason didn't want to tell the real father.

That worried him on a different level. She was a truthful person. A lie like that would only be motivated by a need to protect herself or her family. Had she been attacked or something? Was that why she'd fled?

And what was this crazy story about switching infants? This entire situation was something from a telenovela. None of it made sense, but he could begin to restore order very swiftly.

"Of course," he managed to say. "Where do I have the results sent?"

The administrator returned to the nursery with Octavia's husband. Something in the grim expression worn by Alessandro made Sorcha close her hands more possessively over Enrique. He had a conversation with his wife that Sorcha couldn't quite overhear, though she looked up at the mention of her name. She also caught the name Primo. Octavia had told her Primo was the man Sorcha had seen last night, Alessandro's cousin.

Then the administrator stole everyone's attention.

"We have your blood types." He glanced over a form on a clipboard, then looked up. "I'd like to give you the results, even though they're not conclusive. Ironically, we should have labeled the boys A and B, since that is the blood type they've come back with."

Sorcha listened as Alessandro and Octavia questioned the administrator, confirming their son was type B and Enrique was type A. "If Mr. Montero comes up as an A, we can rule out his fathering this baby." The man nodded at Lorenzo.

"Did you call him?" Octavia asked, turning to look at Sorcha.

Before Sorcha could remind them all that Cesar *was* an A, the administrator said, "We've been in touch with Mr. Montero. He was heading straight to the clinic and his results should be with us shortly."

"Wait. What? You called *Cesar*?" Sorcha

screeched, heart dropping so hard and fast it wound up under her feet, squashed by her slippers as her rocking chair came forward.

Everyone looked at her. She'd confided in Octavia that she and Cesar weren't together, but hadn't admitted he didn't even know he was a father. *This was horrible.*

They needed to get to the bottom of how the babies could have been switched, Sorcha knew that. But Cesar didn't have to know about any of this!

The nursery cleared out again. Octavia's husband left with the administrator to further the investigation. Octavia wore a frown as she rocked her sleeping baby, seeming to be trying to comfort herself.

Sorcha found herself doing the same. Warily she glanced at her mobile. She'd changed her number since leaving his company, but Cesar had messaged.

I just gave a blood sample. Why?

She could hear his coolest, sternest, tell-me-now tone in the short message.

Oh, hell, oh, hell, oh, hell. He was getting married this *weekend*. Should she have told him? How many times had she gone round this mulberry bush of trying to work out the lesser of all the evils? He didn't remember what they'd done. He hadn't called.

He didn't care.

She looked at Enrique's sleeping features, so endearing. Surely Cesar would fall in love as easily as she had? At least she had known her father loved her, even if he hadn't made provisions for them after his death. What would Cesar say, though? His family was the complete opposite of hers: perfectly respectable, yet absent of warmth and the urge for attachment. Was Cesar capable of loving his son? Or would he reject both of them? *That* was what had kept her from calling—not wanting to face his indifference.

Can I call you? she shakily messaged back.

I'll be there in a few hours.

"No-o-o-o…" Sorcha moaned, drawing Octavia's startled glance.

"Is everything all right?" her new friend asked, concerned.

It was too sordid to reveal. "Lost a game," Sorcha lied and tucked her phone away.

What would it do to her to see him again? These months without Cesar had been like a drought, her chest heavy and her limbs weighted as she yearned for him. He hadn't contacted her, though. He didn't feel any of the same pangs.

Hugging their baby, she wished she could spirit her mother across the water to stand by her here in London as effortlessly as Cesar could pilot his own jet from Spain. She desperately needed support to face him.

CHAPTER TWO

THE SKY WAS pewter and drizzling when Cesar parked his car outside the hospital. His phone buzzed again, coming up to twenty messages from his parents. Now his brother was on the trail.

Call me. I want to discuss options.

Cesar dismissed it and thumbed through the rest, marking them to trash.

He'd gone to the clinic with only an abrupt apology, but it had given him time to come to some decisions. On his return, he'd taken Diega aside and explained what had happened.

"We can't marry before the paternity results are in. I'm sorry. Obviously I don't remember doing it, but it's within the realm of possibility that I slept with her. I have to go to London. See her and sort this out."

The concept of having fathered a child was

something he was holding at bay, finding it more than he could take in until the tests confirmed it. However, as much as he wanted to be suspicious of Sorcha's claim, he couldn't discount it. If it turned out he had a son, and he was already married to Diega…

Well, he didn't know how he would react to being a father, but he knew in his gut he didn't want to be married to another woman while he processed something like that.

Disturbingly, Diega hadn't been terribly shocked. She'd tried to talk him out of going. "*Querido*, this isn't a deal-breaker for me. I knew that day that you had had an affair with her. We don't have to put off the wedding because of it."

That had taken him aback. "You said I came to ask if our marriage was really what you wanted," he said. "That I gave you the chance to back out and you didn't have any doubts."

That was why she was calling herself his fiancée even though the banquet and formal announcement had never happened. He hadn't questioned her claim that he'd gone to her for a final, private affirmation that she wanted to move forward. Given all the conflict he'd been feeling in recent months, he had easily seen himself driving out to Diega's home days before they locked themselves into this arrangement, secretly hoping she would call it off.

This sudden new information, that he had confessed to having an affair and had "begged her forgiveness" for it, didn't ring as true.

"She was planning to stay until we married," Diega said. "You didn't want me finding out at some awkward moment in your office, having doubts about your fidelity. I said I would prefer she wasn't lingering in our lives through our engagement and you left to terminate her so we could start our life together without her presence clouding things."

None of that sounded like him, especially the groveling. While he hadn't planned to sleep with anyone else once he and Diega were engaged, he hadn't expected either of them would apologize for anything they'd done previous to their union. Why then, would he have felt such a burning need to go to her after sleeping with Sorcha? Since when did he run from any woman's bed? Lingering and keeping things friendly, leaving on good terms, was his signature move.

If he had stayed with Sorcha, he would remember that day.

Sitting in the parked car, he pinched the bridge of his nose, reminding himself to stop trying to go back in time and change what had happened. He needed to deal with the reality he faced.

But what was that reality?

If Diega had been so offended by his affair

with Sorcha, why hadn't that shone through when they'd spoken of it today? She'd been trying to placate him, encouraging him to believe their wedding could go ahead.

"I understand you might have to take certain measures if the baby proves to be yours, but none of that has to affect plans that have been in the works for *years*."

Her tone had been persuasive, which set off all his inner lie detectors.

He just didn't see himself sleeping with Sorcha after three years of anticipating it, then firing her within hours. He wouldn't do that to her. Over the years, when he had contemplated becoming sexually involved with her, he'd expected it would put an end to her employment with him, but via a lengthy affair that involved cruising on his yacht. Perhaps a visit to his place in Majorca.

Despite entertaining that fantasy more or less daily, he hadn't wanted to lose her at work. She was the best damned PA he'd ever had. So he'd fought his attraction and kept his hands off her for three long, interminable years.

It had been a delicate balance.

And with that much sexual tension built up, it was no surprise he had eagerly pounced if she had proved agreeable, but it didn't make this situation any easier to understand or navigate.

Especially when his phone was blowing up

with messages from his family that he didn't have
to cancel his wedding.

Damn it, it was done. Perhaps too summarily,
and with too much relief, but it was done.

Pocketing keys and phone, he left the car and
strode single-mindedly into the hospital—and
recoiled at the smell.

It was dinner hour. He'd had enough of that generic hospital-food aroma while recovering from
his crash, but determination to get to the bottom
of things propelled him through his repulsion to
ask for Sorcha's room number.

Seconds later he took the stairs in swift leaps,
paced quickly down the hall, had to identify himself to a guard—what the hell was that?—and
finally pushed through her door.

To find her sleeping.

The rush of adrenaline that had been cours-
ing through his arteries since he'd taken the call
from the hospital pooled into a full body burn.
It wasn't so much the angelic look of her that
brought him up short, although that had always
fascinated him when she'd fallen asleep on planes
and curled up in break rooms. She wasn't wearing makeup, which was an oddly vulnerable look
for her, blond lashes and brows barely visible, lips
a pale pink, translucent skin the color of freshly
poured cream.

No, the intravenous tube attached to her wrist

and the wheelchair next to the bed stunned him. A prickling uneasiness stung his back and gut and limbs.

He had visited a woman in hospital after childbirth exactly once: when his sister had been born. His mother had sat on the bed looking as flawless as she had on every other occasion of his life. His six-year-old brain hadn't computed that the baby in the tiny bed on wheels beside her would turn into a child like himself. The room had smelled of flowers and he had not been allowed to take one of the colorful balloons suspended above them. They were just for looks. His parents had been as calmly satisfied as they were capable of being, having produced a third child as scheduled and without setbacks.

There was no baby in Sorcha's clinically barren room, however. No flowers. No balloons.

His heart lurched. He stepped closer to read the labels on the IV bags, one saline, the other an antibiotic. A breast pump had been unpacked from its box and the instructions left on her food tray. She'd been given consommé and gelatin for dinner. Liquids after surgery, he distantly computed, tempted to brush that strand of blond hair from where it slashed in stark contrast across the shadow beneath her eye.

Sorcha had had a baby.

Despite all that had happened, his brain was

still trying to absorb that much and couldn't make sense of the rest. Paternity test? Him? A father?

Three years ago, she had landed her position as his PA with a claim that should have made his fathering her baby impossible.

He'd wanted her from the moment she'd entered his office wearing a pencil skirt and a fitted jacket, both moving like a caress on her slender curves as she walked toward him. She'd had just enough of her throat exposed to avoid being either prudish or inviting. Her blond hair had been held in a simple clip at her nape, her makeup subtly highlighting her pure features. Her smile had only faltered for one blink before it became pleasant and confident. She'd shaken his hand as though they were equals, smoothly pretending her tiny start of sexual awareness hadn't happened.

He'd seen it, however. After a lifetime of always seeing it, he was far more surprised if a glimmer of attraction didn't happen in a woman's face. He was marginally surprised that Sorcha suppressed and set aside her response so well. In his experience, women were either disconcerted by his male energy and became flustered, or quickly tried to find an answering reaction in him by flirting and growing supple with their body language.

Adept at compartmentalizing his own rise of

attraction, particularly in the workplace, he'd taken her hand and invited her to sit, ignoring the sizzle in his blood. But the fact it was there, and so strong, had him deciding against her before she'd bent her narrow waist and pressed her delightfully flared hips into the leather of the interview chair. As much as he preferred his surroundings to be aesthetically pleasing, he'd learned beautiful women could be a detriment in the office, creating politics and causing colleagues to behave badly.

He'd gone through the process of listening to her pitch, however, since he'd promised he would, and she had captured his attention with her wrap-up.

"Finally, I have a solution to a problem that has impacted your productivity for several years."

"What problem is that?" he'd asked with forced patience, thinking drily, *Dazzle me.* He knew all the challenges he faced as he expanded from running his own chemical engineering firm into heading the Montero conglomerate. He'd already made plans for every single pothole in the road.

"You've been running through personal assistants at three and four a year," she said matter-of-factly. "Stability at your base will be paramount as you pick up and run with all your added responsibilities. I'm prepared to offer you a five-year commitment and a promise that I won't sleep with you."

He'd leaned into the backrest of his executive chair to take a fresh assessment of the admittedly competent PA from his father's London office whose brazenness was astonishing. He incinerated powerful men in seconds with this battle-ready stare, but if she was shaking under its laser heat, she was remarkably good at maintaining her demeanor.

"Please take that as a statement of my suitability, not a challenge," she added with a tight smile.

"'Excellent communication skills' also means knowing what *not* to say, Ms. Kelly." He flicked his we're-done glance from her to the door and tapped his keyboard to bring up the next applicant's file.

"Whether you actually slept with your PAs isn't the issue. The perception that you do is an image problem and will persist if you hire one of my older, male competitors." She thumbed toward the roomful of hopefuls beyond his office door. "Hire me, and I'll actively put rumors to rest. Furthermore, I won't throw myself at you or pitch a jealous fit at having to pamper the women who *are* in your life. I won't hit on them, either. Or on any of your associates."

She *was* well-informed. The previous male assistants he'd tried had done exactly that, offering "consolation" to the women he'd broken off with. The married women hadn't been able to keep up with the demands of his travel schedule while the one matronly woman he'd tried had brought a lot of judgment with her. The rest had been a mix of what Sorcha had just described: women given to flirting or openly inviting him or his fellow executives into their beds, searching for a more comfortable situation than working for a living. Even if they hadn't gone that far, they'd too often grown possessive and resentful of his dates.

As for sleeping with any of his PAs, it had happened once in his early years, before he had realized such mistakes could leave him with exactly what Sorcha had just called it: an image problem.

She hadn't won him over that quickly, however.

"I might be inclined to accept your word, Ms. Kelly, if you hadn't slept your way into being granted this interview." Barton Angsley, the middle-aged CEO running the London office, had given her a very glowing reference and pressed hard for her to be considered for this promotion. Despite her solid qualifications, this was an enormous step up in salary and responsibility.

"I don't sleep with anyone to advance my career, Señor Montero. I don't have to," she dismissed without batting an eye.

He had to admit she was solid under pressure.

"Angsley is taking a stress leave because he's

in the middle of an ugly divorce. Infidelity is usually the source of that kind of ugliness, Ms. Kelly. Did you threaten to give his wife the details? Is that why he's so eager to send you to Spain?"

"I don't talk about my employer, ever." Her face became a haughty mask. "As evidenced by the fact you only found out about his divorce when he requested his leave and asked you to interview me. You'll recall that he said they'd been in trouble for nearly a year. I was in the room when he was speaking to you or I wouldn't repeat that much."

Perhaps she'd covered up Angsley's infidelity. Maybe that's why he was so eager to recommend her. Maybe she'd covered his *job*. Cesar recalled a brief comment by his father, as they were discussing possible replacements for Angsley, that the man's work had been exemplary the past few months, despite his personal issues.

Sorcha could be using that as a lever, but she didn't seem prepared to throw her employer under a bus for any reason, even to advance herself.

He'd closed their interview with an assurance that he would give her application due consideration, which had been a lie. He'd had no intention of hiring her, but as her older, male competitors had failed to impress him, he'd found himself thinking about her. Sorcha was the kind of woman he wined and dined. He didn't need the distraction of sexual attraction as he began taking on the role he'd been working toward all his life.

When the time came to make his final decision, however, he'd found himself placing a fresh call to Angsley. He'd learned she had not only rescued some important deadlines on Angsley's last project, avoiding millions in overruns, but she'd also put in her notice once she realized Angsley was using her to cover his cheating.

A few minutes later, he'd found himself dialing her number. "I understand you've been asked to stay on to transition Angsley's replacement, but are working out your notice anyway. Frankly, I would expect more loyalty from an employee seeking to climb our corporate ladder."

A surprised pause, then she said, "Pay me what the position earns and I'd be happy to show his replacement how to do his job. Frankly, given the loyalty I *have* demonstrated, I'd expect not to be overlooked for a promotion just because I'm a woman."

Astute, tough, competent, devoted. *Beautiful.*

"Five years, no sex," he heard himself say.

"Not with you," she confirmed.

"You're underestimating your workload if you think you'll have time for sex with anyone, Ms. Kelly. Be here Monday."

So he found her attractive, he'd mentally

scoffed. He knew how to keep his hands to himself. Nothing would happen between them.

A tickle on her cheek pulled Sorcha from sleep. She brushed at it, bumping against a warm hand that moved away as she opened her eyes.

Cesar.

A sensation of falling hit her, like the mattress was gone and she was falling, falling, falling into an abyss.

While his aqua eyes stayed on her, like he was falling with her as she plummeted, a bird of prey pursuing her, taking his time about snatching her out of the air, letting her feel the tension between temporary avoidance and anticipated capture.

She had expected, if she ever saw him again, that it would be a sweet dawn of sunlit warmth, angels singing and flowers opening. There was none of that. Oh, she was happy, so happy to see him well and strong and looking as fit and commanding as ever. She wanted to smile.

But this man was far too impactful for something so fairy-tale and romantic as merely "happy" feelings. He was a manifestation of a crash of thunder and a streak of lightning, his wide forehead and dark brows stern over those intense eyes that always met hers with such force. His cheeks wore his customary groomed stubble, framing an upper lip that was whimsically drawn and a thickly drawn lower one that had been a sensual delight to suck.

Sex. Oh, this man oozed sex.

She automatically closed her eyes, trying to fight the swell of attraction that lit in her nerves, firing through her system, but it had been far easier to control this response in those three years when she hadn't known how he smelled and tasted. The pattern of hair on his chest flashed into her mind's eye, arrowing a path down his sculpted abdomen to the turgid organ that had speared out shamelessly, thighs tense as he'd stood over her.

Then he'd covered her, powerful arms gathering her beneath his heat as he'd thrust deep, that erotic mouth making love to hers—

"Sorcha." Even his voice made love to her all over again, suffusing her with remembered pleasure.

I'm not ready for this!

She looked through her lashes at him, trying to form some defenses against his effect while searching his expression for the languid, satisfied, tender man who'd kissed her before she'd snuggled against his nudity and fallen asleep.

She closed her eyes again, telling herself she'd fallen asleep in Valencia, had a long, fraught dream and was now waking to...

She opened her eyes to a gaze that had grown

steely, absent of humor or warmth. His jaw was clenched. They weren't even back to his customary good-morning, let's-get-started, businesslike demeanor. This was the man who had dismissed the idea of hiring her at all before he'd even shaken her hand.

"Hello, Cesar," she managed to say, voice husked by sleep and emotion. "It's good to see you've recovered."

"I assumed you expected the worst, given you quit before your contract was up."

A strangled laugh cut her throat, but she was grateful to him for going on the attack. Nothing gave her the ire to fight like being accused of behaving with anything less than integrity.

"I gave you my reasons and you accepted them," she said, reaching for the button to bring up her bed, then wincing as her abdomen protested. She fought not sliding into the footboard as the mattress rose behind her and used one hand to keep the blanket over her chest. "Do you really not remember that week?"

His expression flattened, like a visor had come down to disguise his thoughts and feelings. She had spent three years earning his trust and wasn't used to being shut out like that. Not anymore.

"No. I don't." And he hated it. That much she could tell as she searched his expression.

She didn't know if she was relieved or crushed.

The idea that he might remember their intimacy and hadn't bothered to call had tortured her at her lowest points. His not remembering exonerated him to some extent, but it told her the closeness she'd felt, the connection, was all in her mind. Her memories. As far as he was concerned, they'd never progressed past the incidental touch of fingertips when passing a pen back and forth.

And despite spending way too much time running through the million potential conversations she would have if she ever met him again, she didn't know how to proceed. Especially when, in all of her imagined scenarios, she had at least washed her hair and worn real clothes.

"Are you recovered otherwise?" she asked.

"Completely. What was this reason you gave me for quitting?" he asked with brisk aggression, like his patience had been tested too long. "That you were pregnant?"

She flashed a glance upward. "How would that be possible?" He'd gotten her pregnant *after* she put in her notice.

"I'm no midwife, but it's been eight months since my accident, not nine. You were dating that artist. Is it his?"

Three dates with the painter nearly two years ago, thanks very much to her work schedule, and he still thought it was a thing.

"I went into labor early." She shifted to alleviate the pain in her torso. It was coming from his reaction, though, not her recent surgery. His *lack* of reaction. She'd always thought there was a hint of attraction on his side. He'd said that day that he'd always felt some, but maybe that had been a line.

This was too incredible, not just having to convince a man that he was a father, but that they had had the sex that conceived his son.

"I explained my reasons for quitting and then, um, we slept together. You really don't remember that day?" she persisted.

He stood with his arms folded and his gaze never wavering, but revealed a barely perceptible flinch. "No."

The way he was looking at her, like he was waiting for her to expound on the slept-together details made the pain squeezing her lungs rise to pinch her cheeks. A mix of indignation and agony and plain old shyness burned her alive.

She glanced at the clock, recalling that the nurse had said she'd wake her when Enrique needed to be fed, but that they wouldn't let him go more than four hours. It had been three since he'd last been placed in the incubator.

"When I committed to five years, I didn't know you'd be marrying before that."

"Meaning?"

"Well, as I explained that day…" Oh, that day

had been bittersweet, starting with their customary champagne toast to a project completed. She always loved that time. They so rarely relaxed together, but that was typically when they were both in good spirits. A real conversation about personal things might arise. She'd always felt close to him, then. Valued.

She cleared her throat.

"I realize one of the conditions of your taking over from your father was that you would marry the woman your parents chose for you. I just didn't realize, when you hired me, how the timing would work. That you would get engaged before the five years of transitioning into the presidency were up."

"So you gave notice because I was getting engaged. What did you think was going to happen between us, Sorcha?"

"Nothing!"

"And yet I've been named the father of your newborn. Keep talking."

Pity he'd lost a week's worth of memories instead of that habit of demanding his time not be wasted.

She dragged her gaze off his folded arms and the line of his shoulders. His nostrils were flared. He never lost his temper, but that contained anger was worse. She knew him. She knew with a roiling dread in her belly exactly how much he hated learning of any sort of perfidy. Keeping her pregnancy from him had been a massive act of self-preservation, but there was no way to protect herself now.

"Wives are different from girlfriends." She licked her lips, aware that his sharp gaze followed the action. An internal flutter started up under his attention, but she ignored it. "I wanted to work for you, not her."

"How were you working for her?"

"Little things." She shrugged. "If she wanted tickets for the theater, she asked me to buy them."

"That happened once! You bought them for me all the time."

"Exactly. For you."

He narrowed his eyes. "So when you told me in your interview that you would never become possessive, that was a lie?"

"I wasn't being possessive," she insisted. Okay, she'd been a little bit possessive. Maybe. "It wasn't just buying the tickets. It meant I was expected to put that event into your schedule regardless of anything else you might have planned."

"You rearranged my calendar a hundred times a day anyway. Did you need a raise for this extra responsibility?" That was pretty much what he'd said that day, right down to the facetious tone.

"Changing your timetable on her instruction is

not a responsibility. It's playing politics. *She* was the one being possessive, showing me that she had the power to direct me, which tells me she saw me as a threat. So I chose to remove myself."

"Odd that she would feel threatened, when you, apparently, let our relationship blur into personal?"

"I didn't sleep with you to get at her, if that's what you're suggesting! It just happened. Is that so hard to believe?"

"No," he said with clipped firmness and a hint of self-condemnation.

Her question was supposed to be a knock back, but his response, and the way their gazes locked, kept them firmly in the center of the ring. She could feel him trying to dig past her defensiveness to the truth, trying to see *exactly* how their lovemaking had happened.

Naked and earthy and, in her case, complete abandonment to something that had been building for years.

Her layers of composure began falling away like petals off a rose. A fresh wave of heat rose from her chest, up her throat, into her cheeks. His gaze slid down, scanning like an X-ray, trying to see not through fabric, but through time. He was trying to remember what she looked like, nude and flushed with desire, then pink with recent climax and supreme satisfaction.

The night nurse came in, making them both jerk guiltily.

"Hello," she said cheerily, unaware of the thick sexual tension. "Are you the father? I hope you have identification. The guard at the nursery door will need it. We have strict orders to be vigilant with your two sons."

"Two?" Cesar snapped his head around.

Sorcha caught back a laugh.

"Just one," she assured him. "She means Octavia and I. *Our* sons. The mix-up."

His brows crashed together. "Yes. Explain that."

"Talk while you walk." The nurse brushed him aside so she could assist Sorcha from the bed. "No limo service this time. Dr. Reynolds wants you moving."

Cesar stepped to her other side as she struggled off the edge of the bed.

He reached to flick her gown down her bare thighs before she could, telling her his gaze had been on her legs.

This was such a peculiar situation. She'd slept with him in her mind long before she'd done it in real life, yet the experience remained only in her mind. He didn't share it.

But he brought her shaky grip to his arm to steady her as she stood, acting like intimacy between them was established. She licked her lips, stealing a wary look up at him.

His expression was hard and fierce, impossible to interpret, but when had he ever been easy to read? He was capable of charm, had a dry sense of humor and was incredibly quick to understand almost anything. This situation, however, defied understanding. No wonder he'd retreated to his most arrogantly remote demeanor.

"I was planning to be home when I delivered," Sorcha explained. "But I went into labor early and the cord was in the wrong place. His blood supply would have been cut off if I delivered naturally."

She didn't have a choice about leaning on him. The nurse moved ahead to hold the door into the hall, leaving Sorcha to shuffle from the room by clinging to Cesar's warmth, surrounded in the nostalgic scent of his aftershave.

"They did an emergency C-section and there was a mix-up. Octavia and I knew right away they'd handed us the wrong newborns, but no one believed us. Although..."

She eyed the guards—plural—at the nursery door. One for each baby.

"I guess they believe now that something happened. They're running the DNA tests to confirm it."

"I didn't believe it when I came on shift," the nurse said, tagging her card against the reader to let them into the nursery. "We're all waiting on the results. A mix-up should be impossible."

Sorcha glanced at Cesar to see his mouth tighten again. As the door opened, she held back to let Cesar go in first, asking, "Do you, um, want to see him?"

"Oh, yes," he said darkly, flashing his passport at one of the guards. "If I have a son, I definitely want to see him."

Octavia glanced up from where she was feeding Lorenzo as Cesar swept in. Sorcha only managed a weak, fleeting smile of greeting, too caught up in watching Cesar's reaction to his first sight of Enrique.

Love him, she silently begged.

Cesar stared at the baby inside the dome, stirring and making noises like a fledgling bird. He flashed back again to the memory of his sister, after his mother had brought her home. He had a distinct memory of going in search of his mother to tell her "the baby is crying."

"Yes, they do that," she'd responded. "The nanny will take care of it."

It. With a lifetime of observation behind him, Cesar knew how detached both his parents were from each other and their children. Their union had been a business decision, their conception of heirs a legacy project. On his mother's side, titles and position had to be maintained. His father required sons to run the corporation while he moved into politics. Their daughter was a valuable asset they would leverage into the right position when it came along.

Cesar would swear on a stack of bibles that their dispassion hadn't harmed him. When he'd gone to boarding school, there'd been no homesickness. He'd spoken to his parents exactly as often as he had while sleeping in his own bedroom. As an adult, there were never disagreements, only "further discussion." There was absolutely nothing wrong with the way he'd been raised, or with his parents' expectation that he would be equally practical in his choice of wife and life goals.

Those goals had included a type of payback to Diega's family for stabilizing his situation when the espionage had happened. That mistake still haunted him, making him reluctant to accept he'd made another—one that would keep him from making good on a promise.

Was he a father? He found himself studying Sorcha as a mother. She awkwardly lowered herself into a rocking chair, sighing like she'd run a marathon. Her face was pale, attesting to her weakness, but she smiled as the nurse gathered up the fussing infant and brought him to her.

She greeted the boy with a sultry laugh that tightened Cesar's abs and raised the hairs on the back of his neck. It was like hearing a song you'd first heard on a summer day, taking you back to a time when the weather was perfect and school was out and you had nothing to do for the afternoon.

"You poor thing," she murmured, kissing her baby's cheek, nuzzling him with the sort of affection one saw on nature shows, but that had never been present in his own childhood.

Her easy show of love affected him in a way he couldn't even describe—not sexual, not intellectual. He was fascinated, not sad or happy, but something that teetered between the two emotions.

"Did you miss me? I missed you, too." As her gaze came up, Cesar thought for a stunned moment she was speaking to him. "I named him Enrique," she said, eyes bottomless, lips pink and shiny.

His middle name.

His equilibrium was further thrown off and his palms grew clammy. He wanted to clear his throat, but thought it would seem too revealing. He was suddenly aware of something his sister, the biologist, occasionally said in a dry, disparaging tone to their father. *Emotions are called feelings because you feel them.*

He shook his head, certain his father felt very little. His mother might show some warmth toward an old friend or pout over a favorite vase that toppled and broke, but his father never descended to sentimentality.

He was just like his father. Wasn't he?

"Do you want to hold him?" Sorcha asked huskily.

"Don't you have to feed him?" It was a reflexive response, a quick defense against revealing that he was suffering something he rarely experienced: a profound sense of inadequacy.

He didn't know how to hold a baby. When he had thought about having children, it had always been a distant goal, a step in the process, something he would largely delegate to his wife and whatever staff she hired.

To take care of *it*.

He might as well have slapped Sorcha. She paled and set her chin. "Would you turn around, please?" she asked stiffly.

Because she needed to bare her breast.

If they'd slept together, he'd already seen them, hadn't he?

He turned away, rattled.

He searched his mind for a confirmation of the vision he had conjured thousands of times, when he'd snuck a lecherous peek at her chest. A picture manifested in his mind's eye of creamy swells and taut pink nipples the same shade as her lips. Was that really what she looked like? Or was it just his same detailed fantasy?

He wanted to look, damn it! He wanted to have something, anything, some sign of hope that the lost week was coming back to him. He was a strong, healthy, powerful man who relied on himself. To have his own mind let him down… It was the most gallingly helpless feeling he'd ever experienced. And the doctors didn't expect he'd ever retrieve those memories.

And that thought might have been tolerable if it had been an ordinary week, but no. He had fathered a child during that blackout.

The other mother, Octavia, came to her feet, faltered briefly, then faced them.

"I should tell you… My husband told me that his cousin switched the baby tags during the births. There's…" She shrugged, distress moving over her pretty face as she looked to Sorcha before she glanced back at Cesar with apology. "Jealousy, I guess. Rivalry. The police are involved. I'm sure you'll be asked to make statements. I'm so sorry."

Sorcha, being Sorcha, offered an assurance that it wasn't Octavia's fault.

Cesar couldn't believe what a soft touch she was. Suppose Enrique had gone home with the wrong mother? His child would have been raised by strangers.

It was a chilling thought, one that disconcerted him because deep fury followed it. No one was allowed to steal from him and the idea he might have lost something as precious as his son…

Was Enrique his son?

Was he really wishing it to be true? A tide of… *something* was rising in him.

Octavia moved to tuck her baby into his bed, saying a sleepy good-night as she shuffled out, hand firm on her nurse's arm.

Oddly drawn, Cesar went to the other baby and stared at him, not sure what he was looking for. Babies all looked the same, didn't they?

He wanted another look at the boy Sorcha held. Would he find something of himself in his features? She'd draped a blanket over her shoulder, modestly shielding herself as she nursed.

"When do the DNA results come?" he asked her.

The nurse who had remained in the room looked up from her workstation. "They've rushed the tests. Early next week, we hope."

Cesar clashed his gaze into Sorcha's unreadable one.

He wouldn't believe he'd fathered her baby until the test confirmed it, but he'd never known Sorcha to lie. Not about important things. Not when it came to her family.

The only time she had blown off an afternoon of work, her young niece had gone missing for a few hours. The seven-year-old had climbed onto a wrong bus. Sorcha had been a pale, shaking mess until the little girl had called home from a village two hours from her own.

It had been a disturbing few hours, watching his normally reliable PA fall apart. He hadn't liked it. Not because she'd been inconsolable. She hadn't. She'd gone into a near catatonic state, deeply withdrawn, white as a ghost, only looking at him to ask, "What if...?" He hadn't had answers and he'd been powerless to resolve the issue. He typically mollified women with gifts and compliments and sexual pleasure. The best he'd been able to do was attempt to fly her home.

They'd received the call that the girl was safe before they'd reached the airstrip. Sorcha had hugged him, only then crying a few choked tears, then quickly apologizing and mopping up. Within twenty minutes, they'd been back to normal, working productively, pretending the embrace hadn't happened, but he'd never forgotten the intensity of her emotions.

Or the feel of her pressed to his front, her shoulder so small under his hand, her blue jacket thin enough he'd felt the suppleness of her back. She didn't wear perfume. Her scent was subtle, like those complex notes he used to try to identify with his father's vintner. Crushed flower petals? A hint of anise?

His mind had turned to sex in that moment of

holding her, not that making love to her was so very far from his private bank of fantasies from the moment he saw her in the morning to when he fell asleep at night. From her interview onward, he had accepted that he wanted her and couldn't have her, so he'd briefly returned her embrace, then set her away.

That time.

But not the next time he'd held her, apparently.

He sighed impatiently, wanting to believe that if Sorcha had put his name down as the baby's father for any reason beyond the truth, it was a damned good one. Not just money, either, no matter the fortune he had. Because if it was his fortune she was after, she wouldn't have kept the baby a secret right up until the moment he was about to marry someone else.

Why then…?

"Why," he said aloud, moving over to her and switching to Valencian so they could speak with some privacy. "If I'm his father, why did I find out like this? Why didn't you say something sooner? Why not stay and force me to face it? Why not ask me for support?"

She'd always been good under pressure, rarely revealing her thoughts or feelings, but a vulnerable anger flashed across her expression.

"I tried to see you. I asked your father a dozen times, went to the hospital, but I wasn't allowed up." Her face hardened. "It was a difficult time for your family and you were in very bad shape. I wanted to be compassionate about that. When I heard you'd lost your memory…" She searched his gaze as though still having trouble believing it.

So did he. He flinched, angered all over again at his own fallibility. He turned away.

"The circumstances weren't ideal," she continued behind him. "You were engaged to Diega even if it wasn't official—" She sighed. "We talked a lot that day and you confided your reservations about marrying. I thought it meant you were deciding against going through with it or I never would have…"

He glanced back to see her dip her head, smoothing her brow with a troubled finger.

He strained his brain, searching for what he might have said to her. Yes, he'd had reservations about his engagement from the time he was twenty and his mother identified Diega as a suitable future wife, but his parents had a perfectly civil, successful arrangement. This was how his family conducted themselves. You didn't achieve long-term professional success by chasing "love." You built a satisfying environment by partnering with people of similar minds and means. He had resolved himself to doing his part in expanding the family's standing and fortune.

And doing right by Diega's family.

So he had ignored the feeling in the pit of his gut and approved the plan to engage himself when his mother had pressed him.

Privately he acknowledged that in those weeks leading up to the party, he had begun to feel like the walls were closing in. He wasn't sure why he would have opened up to Sorcha about it, though. Postcoital lowered defenses or not, that was a more personal thing than he would typically confide even to her.

"I wanted to tell you first, obviously," she said with a despairing sigh. "But I couldn't get in to see you. What was my alternative? Tell your father? He would have thought, at best, that I'd done this on purpose. I didn't, Cesar. We used a condom. It failed. I can see you barely believe me. Your father wouldn't have, either." She looked away, cheekbones flushed with indignation while sadness tugged at the corners of her pretty mouth.

What had it felt like to kiss her? As good as he'd always imagined?

His hand closed into a fist and a fresh wave of feeling cheated gripped him.

"I didn't expect you *could* believe me, if the memory was gone. In every scenario, when I imagined convincing you or anyone else that Enrique was yours, I saw myself being paid off. I don't want your money." Her eyes met his, as steady and truthful as he'd ever seen her. "The only reason I gave your name on the forms here was because it was an emergency. If I hadn't made it through the surgery, I didn't want my mother burdened with the cost of raising Enrique. At that point, yes, I would hope you would open your wallet."

A chill moved through him at her saying "hadn't made it through." He brushed aside the thought of such a disturbing outcome and latched on to her other shocking admission. "So you never would have told me?"

She looked down, chewing the inside of her lip. "Never is a long time." Her gaze flicked up uncertainly. "Enrique might have had questions. I was going to wait and see."

He was flabbergasted.

He reminded himself the boy might not be his, but damn it, he'd spent three years entrusting Sorcha with confidential information, decisions that affected stock prices, personal opinions that he hadn't shared with anyone else… Aside from leaving him when he'd been at his lowest point, she'd never let him down. From their first meeting, she'd been disarmingly frank, in fact.

So had he. She knew exactly how he felt about people who lied and kept secrets and messed with his scrupulously ordered life.

"I'm not 'waiting to see,'" he growled, aware that despite a lack of hard evidence he *did* believe her. "I called off my wedding."

She took that in with a stunned expression, then recovered with a shaken little shrug. "Well, I didn't ask you to. I don't have designs on you myself, if that's what you're worried about." She made the claim firmly enough, but her lashes trembled as she flicked another look at him.

Like she was trying not to betray that, on some level, she'd entertained the idea.

That didn't surprise him. He was a rich, titled, healthy man. All women took his measure and often made a play. According to his sister, it was basic biology. He had the kind of power and resources that appealed to fertile women looking for a mate to provide for her young.

And that was what Sorcha ought to expect if he was indeed the father of her child.

"Really," he said skeptically, folding his arms, taken aback, but when had Sorcha *not* surprised him?

"Really," she affirmed. "If you want to make provisions for your son, that's your choice, but I will proceed as if I'll be supporting Enrique alone."

Of course he would support his child. That wasn't even something he had to consciously decide, it was such a no-brainer. What kind of man failed to provide the basics of life to his off-spring?

The natural progression of that thought—*how* he would provide for Enrique—was a more complex decision he was holding off contemplating.

All his life, he'd had a perfect defense against ambitious women: he was tied to an arranged marriage of his parents' choosing. Now, for the first time in his life, he was free of that encumbrance, yet morally bound to at least consider marriage to Sorcha.

If Enrique was his.

That odd rush of longing for the boy to be his rose again, stronger this time, bunching his muscles with anticipation as though he could physically fight for the outcome he wanted.

"I wasn't trying to trap you that day," Sorcha continued, brow wrinkling. "We had some champagne and talked about personal things. I felt—" She flushed and swallowed, but forced her chin up to meet his gaze with defiance. "I felt like we were friends. That's why I slept with you." Her expression darkened to one of hurt and betrayal. "But when I came to the hospital to see you, Diega told me you called me your last hurrah."

Sorcha's gaze took a scathing sweep that sliced across him. *Slash, slash, slash*, like Zorro's sword dissecting him into pieces.

"She said I had become a challenge. A

conquest—her word—that you couldn't stand to let get away. I've been so comforted all these months, Cesar, knowing you had a good laugh at my expense right before you nearly died."

CHAPTER THREE

SHE POLITELY KICKED Cesar out after that. Enrique needed to go to bed and so did she. She was exhausted emotionally and physically. Cesar was too much on her best day and she was not at her best.

Still, the fact he hadn't tried to defend himself before he departed wrenched her soul from her body.

She was hurting. Furious. He wanted to know why she hadn't told him they'd made a baby? Because it hadn't meant anything to him. If it had, if *she* had, he would have called her before now.

She took a shaken breath, wondering if he would come back.

Don't be stupid, she berated herself. She'd given him a get-out-of-jail-free card. *Note to self: don't gamble unless you're prepared to lose.*

Swallowing back her misery, she resigned herself to raising Enrique alone, already missing Cesar. She had missed him all these months, missed his dynamic pursuit of his goals, his easy command of any situation, his bursts of enthusiasm for a fresh project and his nod of satisfaction over a job well done.

She would keep missing him *so much*.

Except...

He was different. He'd always had that air of contained energy, but there was a higher, colder wall around him, not that he'd ever been the most demonstrative person. His entire family was like that: aloof and reserved. She had always thought it ironic that, despite their Latin roots, the Monteros were devoid of the clichéd warmth and short fuse one was taught to expect from the Spanish.

Was it the situation? Or had the accident changed him in a fundamental way? Because by the time they'd opened up to each other that day in Valencia, she'd moved from intimidation through hero worship to falling in love with the man she'd come to know. She had thought she'd known him quite well, despite the fact he hadn't divulged more to her than, she suspected, anyone else he'd ever confided in. She had simply observed.

Her heart lurched as she settled herself in her bed, thinking of all the small ways he'd proven to be more than a focused businessman governed by logic and the scientific method. In her three years of working for him, he'd revealed himself to be caring enough to catch a loose dog off a highway so it wouldn't get hit. He'd let her in on his secretive experiments with metallurgy that didn't always have a practical purpose, he just had to *know*. He bordered on being a nerd about those things, actually, bemusingly eager to report his findings.

And even though he had a dry wit, he rarely laughed. Except around her. She actively tried to make him laugh, just to hear his surprised snort.

Sorcha swallowed, recalling how they'd split that bottle of champagne that day, congratulating each other. That was another thing she adored about him. He acknowledged her contribution, never taking all the glory for himself.

Tomorrow, she had been thinking as they clinked glasses that afternoon. Tomorrow she would draft up his thank-you letters to the various department heads. He would go through each one, noting specific areas of achievement and offering his appreciation. It wasn't sentimental, he'd assured her the first time he'd given her the task. "Research shows that positive reinforcement achieves better results than negative feedback. Moving forward, the teams will be doubly motivated to strive for excellence.

"Nice work with the press," he'd said to her as they sipped their champagne, adding the warning, "It will get worse."

"I know." His father was moving into politics and every level of media, from serious journalists to paparazzi, was turning over rocks, eager for something to crawl out. But with one verbal pat on the back from her exalted boss, Sorcha mentally dug in, determined to keep earning his approval.

For a moment they'd shared a comfortable silence. The sun had painted muted patches of light on the oriental carpet, shining through the coated glass of the windows. His phone had chimed on his desk and he'd had his guard down enough that he didn't disguise the twist of dismay that contorted his mouth before he controlled it.

Only his family had his direct number, but he didn't rise or ask her to fetch it.

Oh, right. Diega Fuentes, his soon-to-be fiancée, also had the number.

Cesar topped up their sparkling glasses, ignoring the call.

Leaning forward on the sofa, Sorcha set down her glass, taking advantage of Cesar's attention on his placement of the bottle back into its ice bucket to memorize his profile, so sharp and proud. His big shoulders shrugged briefly as he settled back into his chair. He lifted his feet onto the coffee table and crossed his ankles, releasing a contented sigh.

This was their private ritual, this brief celebration of closing out a project. In a moment his mind would turn to the stages of all the other projects they were juggling and she would set her phone to record his musings. She might rise to fetch a notebook or search out a file or drawing as they began prioritizing their next series of tasks.

But not yet. Right now, this was their downtime.

And she had some business of her own to address.

"You have something to say," he noted, watchful beneath those lazily drooped eyelids, making her feel self-conscious. When had he learned to read her?

She swallowed. This was the moment she'd been waiting for and it was harder than she'd expected. Her throat tightened and the words came up with a little rasp, dragging a barb. "I have to put in my notice."

"Did you mishear me? I said you did well with the press."

She smiled, but it didn't stick. *I'm serious*, she telegraphed.

He lifted disdainful brows. "You promised me five years."

"I did," she admitted.

"Something to do with your family?"

"No." His question surprised her. Apart from

the incident with her niece, she hadn't realized he'd noticed how important her family was to her, especially given how indifferent he seemed toward his own. "No, it's…" She hadn't figured out how to approach this without coming off as insulting him, his family, his attitude toward marriage and his intended. "You know how sometimes you ask me to tell a white lie to a woman you're dating, to say you've left the building when they drop by unannounced? Or to take the fall if you forget to call? That kind of thing?"

"I didn't put that in your job description. You did." He took a healthy swallow of sparkling wine, expression shuttered, all his attention on her.

He certainly took advantage of her willingness to send flowers, pay bills, cosset and reassure the revolving door of women he dated.

"I did," she agreed. "Because I took a job working as PA to a bachelor and that's a sort of job hazard. Working for a married man is different." She looked at her hands to remind herself to keep them still because it made her a little sick to think of him married to that ice queen Diega Fuentes. "You either become friends with his wife, in which case you can't lie to her for any reason, even if your boss asks you to, or she sees you as an extension of his job—that thing that takes him away from her. And she makes it hard for you to do your work effectively."

"You think Diega will make your job hard for you? Because I would never ask you to lie to her."

"Wouldn't you?" Asking the question, especially in that low, quietly challenging tone, was a gamble. It was the same high-stakes candor she'd used to land this job and tried not to overuse. But this was important.

With trepidation, she lifted her gaze and had to steel herself against stammering out an apology. He was giving her the death glare, the one that made muscled construction workers armed with nail guns take a step back in caution.

"Keep talking, Sorcha, and the termination will come from this side of the table."

"Either way I'm leaving, so I have nothing to lose in speaking my mind, do I?" She picked up her drink and drew deeply on the bubbly liquid that evaporated in her mouth, but she didn't say anything more, not wanting things to end badly after such a good three years.

He dropped his feet to the floor and sat forward, taking up his hard-negotiator stance, drink going onto the table with a decisive *clink*. "Surely you could come up with a better reason if you're looking for a raise. How much did you have in mind?"

"I don't want more money."

"Your workload will lighten, you know. She'll arrange for my dry cleaning to come home. Tell me the real reason we're having this conversation."

As a child, after failing to change minds with unceasing logic or heated emotion, she had learned to keep it simple. Make her statement and dig in. She was probably too stubborn for her own good, but she didn't backtrack or waffle, never stammered out excuses or defenses. If she messed up, she owned it. If she thought Cesar was making an error in judgment, she told him. Once.

He valued all of this about her. He'd told her during reviews.

She also knew how to let silence make a point. She'd learned that from the master sitting across from her.

"You're serious?" he demanded after a long, charged minute. "You want to quit because I'm getting engaged? We won't marry until next year."

"I'll stay through the hiring and training period. Once you've set a date, I'll work until the Friday before your wedding, if you want me to stay that long."

"This is unacceptable. You promised me five years." He picked up his glass and glowered at her. "I'm so tempted to fire you right now, you have no idea."

She picked up her own glass and sat back, already melancholy. She prided herself on her reliability and hated to let him down. If she had thought he loved Diega— No, that would be worse. She would quit even faster if he fell in love. She frowned, wishing she wasn't so infatuated with him. None of this would bother her.

"Why do you think I'll ask you to lie to her?" he demanded in a low growl.

She took heart from his question. Sometimes she let herself believe they were friends, especially when he did this, asked for her thoughts. He might not be in love, but talking about his forthcoming marriage still seemed profoundly personal. She couldn't help but read in to it, believing he valued her opinion.

"The thing that strikes me," she said carefully, "is how different you are with her. I've seen you with women, Cesar." She offered a tolerant smile. Did she resent those women? Hell, yes, but she'd known he was a playboy before she'd interviewed for the job. "I can make all the judgments I want about the quantity of women you date, but you always appear to *like* them. To be genuinely attracted. When you see Señorita Fuentes coming, you give her the same look you wear when greeting a tax auditor."

"I don't lie to tax auditors, either," he said flatly, looking away, mouth twisting with disgust. "Most people tell me I'm difficult to read, you know."

"You are. But I know you."

"Do you." His gaze swung back to hers and something in the sudden connection made her heart skip.

"I like to think so," she disclosed.

"Then you know this is how my life must go. You know about the industrial spying?"

"Yes." She'd read what she could find online about it. The court case had gone on for years, but the intellectual property that had been stolen hadn't been something that could be reclaimed. Once Pandora's box had been opened, there was no restitution.

"It was my fault. I was using my father's money, gambling that my work would pay back the coffers with interest. The work was stolen, the investment went bust and the legal bills were horrendous. Yes, we eventually retrieved a fraction of that in the settlement, but it was a pittance against the fortune that we should have had. We could have faced bankruptcy if not for Diega's family helping us refinance. They stepped up because we've always had this understanding between our families that we would be joining forces when the time was right."

Sorcha couldn't remember him ever directly referencing the espionage. The closest he'd come was mentioning the name of his first company, "the one that was lost." Each word of what he'd just said had been bitten off with a gnash of his teeth, bitter and filled with self-recrimination.

"If I've taken advantage of my freedom, enjoyed a 'quantity' of women," he said, quoting her pithily, "it's because I've always known my opportunity to do so was finite. I don't intend to cheat on her, Sorcha. You won't be expected to lie."

She smiled. His tenacity was so predictable. "My notice still stands."

"Because you think she'll make it hard for you to do your job." He shook his head. "If this was a love match, perhaps, but our marrying is a business decision. She knows my work is my priority. My life."

That statement struck her as alarmingly hollow. Sorcha gleaned a lot of satisfaction from her work, but a huge part of that satisfaction came from providing for the people she loved. Her *life* was her family. And Cesar, she added silently. Her heart was so misguided.

"Cesar, my father married for those sorts of practical reasons," she confided, clearing her throat because her soul was still pulled and frayed by the circumstances after his death. He'd failed them, not just financially, but by leaving them humiliated. She still nursed a deep hurt over that. "He needed the money to keep his family's estate intact. Then he fell in love with my mother."

Cesar sat arrested for a moment. "I didn't know that about you."

"That I'm illegitimate? The product of infidelity? I don't advertise it." She actively tried to hide it, in fact, but for his greater good she would reveal a little of her deepest shame. "I'm saying there are pitfalls to what you're contemplating."

"Love?" He finished his drink and set down his glass, then pulled the dripping bottle from the ice bucket and motioned for her to lean forward with her half-empty glass. "Not something my family subscribes to. You must have noticed?"

This was the most intimate conversation they'd ever had, which was why Sorcha held her glass to be refilled and sat back to let it continue.

"I've noticed. I wasn't sure you had. Noticed, I mean." He definitely didn't subscribe to love. Women were for entertainment and he did his best to make that a two-way transaction, but emotions were not on the invoice.

He didn't flinch, but there was a flash of...she wasn't sure what.

"The way you talk about your family." His face smoothed to hide his thoughts, but there was still something watchful beneath his neutral expression. "Our family is a business. I prefer it, but I sometimes wonder what it would be like to be close like that."

"It's nice," she informed him, feeling a sudden, misguided urge to convert him. Occasionally there were birthday wishes that required her to take a moment from her busy schedule. He had walked in on her chatting over her tablet a time or two, when she was supposed to be off the clock but they were both working late. She'd flown her sister to Paris on points, as a graduation gift, when she and Cesar had been there for meetings. He'd personally paid for their dinner, but had gone on his own date without so much as laying eyes on her sister. If anything, she had imagined he found her tight relationship with her mother and sisters an annoying distraction from her work.

"Some of us could probably do with thinking more practically in our choices with mates," she added, thinking of her mother's involvement with her father.

"*You* certainly could. How is your artist?" he asked, surprising her.

"Why do you say it like that? *Your artist.* Like it's a joke. You've dated a painter, too," she reminded him.

"I've also dated stockbrokers. You've had one

serious relationship since I've known you and it's the most impractical man you could find."

"He's nice," she explained on a shrug. If absentminded. She'd only accepted his invitation to cook her dinner because she'd been wallowing in self-pity at being devoid of a social life. Cesar found out when he'd called her in the middle of their date. She'd had to explain why she couldn't run to her computer to transfer a file.

"You're already sending money home, Sorcha. Don't take on another dependent for the sake of feeling 'loved.'" The emotion was an unviable fantasy, he seemed to say.

"I wasn't in love with him. And we're no longer seeing each other. The demands of my job make dating impossible," she added pointedly.

"Good. He struck me as too sensitive and probably insecure in bed. You need a man with the confidence to take control so you can finally give it up."

She blushed. "We *are* getting personal today, aren't we? Are you drunk?"

"You started it," he admonished. "And no, I'm not. But I'm in a mood to drink myself blind now. You've ruined what started out as a very good day." He chucked back the contents of his champagne glass and rose to move to the bar, taking out the Irish whiskey she'd turned him onto drinking.

"Do you want the truth, Cesar?" She bent her knees as she twisted on the sofa, bringing her feet off the floor and hooking her elbow over the sofa back to face him.

"Probably not," he muttered, not looking up from pouring.

"I…care for you." It was as much of an admission to the depth of her feelings as she was willing to risk. "I don't want to watch you live with a bad decision."

His gaze came up. "You said you'd never get jealous." Rather than annoyed, he sounded smug.

"Hardly. I just don't want to watch you make a mistake. So I'm leaving."

"Do *you* want the truth, Sorcha?" He came back with two wide-bottom glasses, both neat, offering one to her as he settled onto the sofa beside her, angled to face her.

"Probably not," she muttered.

"I always thought that if you left before the five years were up, it would be because we slept together. The fact my mother and Diega have pushed this marriage into our time line annoys me. I was counting on sleeping with you in seven hundred and fifty days or so."

She almost dropped her glass. "You *are* drunk."

"I'm not. Just being honest. Now you be as honest as I know you are. Don't you wonder what we'd be like together?"

She slid him a glance, astonished that she was having this conversation with her boss. Once he'd hired her, they'd had a tacit agreement to never speak of her vow again. The odd time when a rumor floated that she and Cesar were an item, she quashed it with her I-don't-have-to-use-those-tactics speech.

They had kept things strictly professional. Occasionally he'd told her she looked nice and once or twice he'd steadied her with a hand under her elbow, when crossing an icy runway or uneven pavement. Even when she'd hugged him after her niece was found, he'd gently but firmly moved her away afterward. Given his seeming indifference to her being female, she had assumed all the sexual awareness was on her side.

"We're being honest?" she confirmed, wondering if she was tipsy since she was going along with this inappropriate conversation. "Your women always look happy. Of course, I wonder what it's like to date you," she said with a blasé tone that was completely manufactured. "But I often wonder what *dating* is like."

"Keep trying to make me feel guilty," he said. "I won't."

He was so close, smelling deliciously raw and masculine, so comfortable with his arm across the back of the sofa behind her, his knee hitched up near her hip. This was how she'd seen him with countless women: relaxed, confident in his own skin. Attentive. Like she was the only thing he was thinking about in this moment.

Maybe he was thinking about sex.

With her.

A flutter of excitement contracted her belly, making her feel prickly and sensual. She found herself doing the hair-play thing, tucking a strand behind her ear, subtly flirting under his regard.

A faint smile touched his mouth. He knew. He was too experienced not to read how she was reacting.

Then a shutter came down. He straightened, sitting forward, setting his glass on the table, bracing his elbows on his knees as he released a sigh. "I keep telling myself to take Diega to bed, to be sure we'll work, but…" He shrugged. "It won't matter. We still have to marry."

"But you don't want to?" She sat forward, too, nearly thigh against thigh, her own glass going onto the table next to his. "Cesar, you're a grown man."

"With responsibilities, Sorcha." He turned his head, shoulders heavy and back bowed by the weight of his obligations.

"Is all of this really going to come crashing down if you don't marry her?" She waved a hand at the office, beautifully decorated on a budget of over six figures, where deals were cut for tens of millions on a weekly basis.

"My family is building an empire, not a rose garden. I have a role. I agreed to all the conditions."

"Fine. Go against your gut and live with the consequences." She threw that out with a shrug.

"Where do you find the gall to talk to me like this? I've never understood why I put up with it," he muttered, but he wasn't angry. Disgusted with himself maybe. "My gut decisions are always supported by reason. Backing out would have to be driven by logic. There are a hundred solid facts that make marrying Diega a smart choice."

"And your happiness isn't reason enough to support a different choice? What would happen if you refused to marry her? No one will be burned at the stake. Surely you're in a position now to make reparation for whatever they gave you? Or to weather your father disinheriting you? What is the worst that will happen, Cesar?"

His mouth stayed tight for a long moment before he snorted and took up his glass for a quick swallow. "Indeed. Will my mother stop loving me? She never started." He set down the glass again with a hard clip of glass on glass. "But much of what I now control could move into my brother's hands."

"Really? After you've proven yourself to be so good at it? I don't believe it."

"This all must look very simple from the outside." His gaze came up from her white nail beds where she gripped his arm. His voice lowered a shade into something intimate. "Would you stay in your job if I refused to marry her? Is that why you're trying to convince me?"

"Would you refuse to marry her if I canceled my notice?" she scoffed, pretty much making it a dare. She didn't mean that much to him. She knew she didn't. Given all he stood to gain, he *couldn't* call off his marriage just to sleep with his secretary.

"If you let me have you, I might. You would be surprised what I would do for that privilege." He was looking at her mouth.

Her heart began to pound.

"Cesar..."

"I need to know what it's like to kiss you, Sorcha." He brought up a hand, one strong finger tracing a line under her jaw to a point under her chin.

Breathe, she thought, but couldn't make her lungs work. She was frozen in hot ice, mouth parting as he angled his head and leaned to cover her lips with his.

This was what he meant by her needing a man who could take control. As the oldest of four in a single-parent home, she'd been an adult from an early age, taking care of her siblings, then helping with the breadwinning. She easily shouldered responsibility—even for her own pleasure—but from the first touch, Cesar let her know he was more than willing to give her anything she desired.

There was no hesitation in his kiss, only command. He didn't overwhelm, wasn't forceful, but his kiss had the same quality as his voice or his directing hand. We're going *here* and this is how we'll get there. Come with me. I'll show you.

She softened under his thorough kiss, liking the light abrasion of his stubble. Her lips clung to his and her hand climbed his arm and found his shoulder. She tried to maintain her balance as they sat there, side by side, quietly devouring each other.

He shifted, gathered her and drew her into his lap. Just like that. Strong and sure, making his intention clear, right down to the bulge pressed against the cheek of her bottom.

They broke off their kiss, looked into each other's eyes. This was the point when she was supposed to remind him they had an agreement. He was her boss—if he was serious about refusing to marry Diega.

You would be surprised what I would do for that privilege.

His neck was hot against her palm and the trace of his fingers against her thigh triggered a rush of tingling need into her loins. She had imagined making love with him so many times, had longed for it in the dead of night, tossing and turning while he made love to other women.

This time he would make love to her. She would know what it felt like to feel his touch, to bask in his attention. Her sex life *was* dismal, she'd reasoned. She hadn't gone all the way with that dumb artist. Their bit of fooling around had been great for him and left her feeling nothing. She ached for a good experience.

She wanted sex, wanted Cesar, yearned to feel even closer to him than she already did. She wanted to make love with him.

Stay with him.

She moved her hand to the back of his head and lifted her mouth to meet his kiss.

CHAPTER FOUR

CESAR DIDN'T GET back to the hospital until late the next morning. By then he'd had a number of tablet conversations with his mother and brother— *you know she'll tell me to marry Diega if you don't*—and finally, the unsurprising arrival of his father.

The consensus seemed to be that the situation did not warrant calling off a wedding, even if he could be sure the baby was his.

Their attitude was almost as frustrating as Sorcha's accusation yesterday, when she'd called him out for using her, then asked him to leave. She'd been pale with dark circles under her eyes, the nurse standing by with one of those paper cups full of pain pills. He'd had to give her the opportunity to rest that she needed.

And he hadn't known how to counter her accusations. He didn't remember what he'd said to Diega about her, but he'd obviously confessed that they'd slept together.

It was all such a frustrating mess, but the signpost for the way forward hinged on whether Enrique was his.

He returned to the hospital in a driven state of mind, going directly to the nursery for a long, proper look at the boy, determined to find proof.

Sorcha was there, putting the baby down, her expression relaxed and tender until she glanced up and saw him. Her smile fell away. "I assumed you'd jetted back to Spain."

One sharp look had her sealing her lips, but her chin went up. She wasn't cowed. He'd always found her inability to be intimidated refreshing—it allowed him to be who he was without signing up for sensitivity training—but engaging in battle with him at this precise moment was not her best move.

He came across and slid his attention to the baby, determined that if there was something of himself in the boy, he'd see it.

Sorcha's hands curled into loose, pale fists against the glass over the tiny bed as she waited out his study in silence. Were those miniature brows similarly shaped to the rest of the males' in his family? That button nose and those round cheeks were too soft to bear any resemblance to anyone but another baby. That mouth was Sorcha's. Hair? Similar in color to his own, he supposed, but inconclusive. Ears?

Finding visible proof of paternity was like trying to locate the memory of having conceived him—it wasn't there. He'd spent the night trying to recall making love to her, driving himself crazy, coming up empty.

He was a scientific man, never one to accept anything less than factual evidence. He certainly didn't take anyone at his word. He'd been burned by that when his "friend," the abrasive specialist, had hacked into his network and stolen a year's worth of experimental data and testing results.

Since the crash, however, since losing a vital piece of his memory, he *had* to take certain things on faith. He had no choice but to believe what people told him he had said or done during that time. There was nothing to counter it but gut instinct.

His gut was telling him to trust the PA who'd never let him down.

"If you have another story, Sorcha, now is the time to tell it," he said, lifting his gaze from the baby. He stood at a cliff face, ready to step off of it. On her word.

She stilled, face solemn. For all her natural beauty, her intelligence was really one of her best features. A flicker of despondency moved across her expression. "I imagine I'll wish I did, but I don't." A spasm of hurt tightened her expression. "Why? What are you going to do?"

"Let's take this to your room, where we'll have some privacy."

They were speaking Valencian and there was only the one nurse in here, but Sorcha nodded. He held the door for her and paced slowly alongside her as she leaned on the wall all the way to her room.

Her IV was gone and she was moving better, standing straighter, but was still pale. She sighed with relief as she settled on the bed and he brought the blanket up over her legs. A big arrangement of flowers had arrived to give her windowsill a splash of color.

He frowned, mind jumping to that artist of hers.

"Octavia's mother sent it to her. She already had one from her husband and knew I told my mother to save her money for baby clothes, so she gave that one to me."

Right. Some grandparents sent flowers to congratulate a new mother when she delivered an heir into the family.

What did Enrique's grandfather send? Cesar reached into his shirt pocket.

"From my father," he said, offering it.

She didn't take it, only looked at the amount. "My, he does value Señorita Fuentes, doesn't he?" She turned away to reach for her glass on her side table and sipped from the straw. The color in her high cheekbones was the only indication of her reaction.

He'd always liked that collected demeanor of hers. He'd liked far too many things about her, and even today, mind dull and body aching from not sleeping, when he was trying to recover from having his mind blown apart, there was a piece of him that just wanted to crawl into that bed with her and *have* her.

It struck him that he hadn't felt a rush of attraction like this since before his crash. Desire for sexual release was always there, like hunger or thirst. But last night, as he'd tried to manifest an image of having Sorcha, he'd mentally ridden her hard. He never had those sorts of fantasies about Diega. In fact, since waking up "engaged," he'd more or less put his inner sex animal into a kennel and told him to shut up.

The beast was snarling to life now, pouring predatory heat through Cesar's veins. Desire gathered in painful pools at his groin. He was having enough trouble working through the facts without trying to hide an erection!

He left the certified check on her bed and moved to the window, pushing his fists into his pockets. "The joining of our family with Diega's is something both sides have wanted for a long time," he said in explanation. "My father isn't ready to let it go."

Despite a lifetime of witnessing his parents' indifference, he was disturbed by how cold-bloodedly they were behaving. It wasn't that they didn't believe Sorcha's claim. They didn't *care*. "He wants me to marry Diega regardless of this…" He gestured to the hall. *"Hiccup,"* he said with disgust at their attitude.

"Obviously," Sorcha said with a nod at the paper he'd left near her knee.

"Are you going to accept it?" It was a test, he had to admit it. He had long-standing trust issues, and mentally willed her to rip it up. If he knew her as well as he believed he did, she would never consider family a commodity from which she should profit.

She glared at the check for a long moment before her shoulders drooped and she released a defeated sigh. "It would be stupid not to tuck that into an account for emergencies," she said reluctantly. "Or whatever Enrique might need down the road. I would hate him to think his father hadn't cared enough to provide for his future. That's a horrible feeling."

Cesar turned to face her, startled by what he thought she was saying, but finding himself folding his arms, astonished by the more pertinent revelation. "You think I should marry Diega while you raise my son alone?"

"What other option is there?" She held up a

quick finger of warning. "If you suggest taking him to live with you and Diega, there will be blood shed, right here, right now." The tip of her finger went to the open spot on the floor.

A bitter smile pulled at his lips. Did she really see him as the type to take a baby from a mother who knew how to love and give him to a cold fish like his own?

But if not that kind of man, what kind *was* he?

He scowled, unsure of his ability to be anything but a peripheral figure the way his own father had been. He hadn't expected to be so distant from his offspring that he was out of his son's life completely, however. He'd spent the night running all the scenarios and while he didn't care that his parents weren't the most demonstrative people, there was something very alluring about offering his child a more nurturing upbringing.

Then there was the fringe benefit: Sorcha. He wanted her. If he was going to be supporting her and their child, they might as well go all the way.

He met Sorcha's belligerent gaze, as she waited for him to enlighten her, but how could this be a mystery to her? She knew how he reacted to someone trying to take what was his.

"His parents could raise him together," he said.

* * *

Sorcha was glad she was sitting because her heart stopped then kicked with a hard beat of shock, making her woozy. *As husband and wife?*

No. She wasn't so silly as to hear a proposal in that statement. He might have called off his wedding, but that was just a postponement. Wasn't it?

"You, um, want to move to Ireland with me?" she asked.

"It's good you're keeping your sense of humor," he said with a faint, patronizing smile. "No. We'll marry and live in Spain."

Another breathtaking spasm squeezed and released her heart. She tried to swallow and couldn't.

"You want to marry me," she managed to say. "What about—" She waved at the check. "I thought this meant you're marrying Diega after all. Was it this romantic when you proposed to her, by the way? I'm sorry, that's cruel. You probably don't remember because you were in a coma. At least I'm awake. Count your blessings, Sorcha!" she babbled, hysterical laughter rising in her throat.

Cesar didn't move, his face stony. "There are times, Sorcha, when that runaway tongue of yours really ought to be held firmly between those pretty white teeth."

"What do you want me to say?" she cried. "Thank you? Apparently your brides are interchangeable. I've never felt that way when contemplating my eventual husband."

"My children are not," he stated, tone as hard as his expression. "Interchangeable. And he had better be my son, Sorcha. If those tests come back telling me I've been had, I won't be happy."

"As opposed to now, when you're ecstatic?"

"Less sarcasm once we're married, hmm? More sweetness."

She snorted. "We're not getting married, Cesar."

"Sorcha," he said in that terrible voice he used when he was about to annihilate someone. She had always excused herself from the room so the poor sod wouldn't have a witness to his or her dressing-down.

Her stomach curdled, but she tightened militant fingers into the blanket across her waist and said, *"No."*

He came over to clench his hands around the rail of her bed.

"You know how I feel about thieves," he said in that deadly tone. "You were going to keep my son from me. *You* were going to do that to *me*. I may never forgive you for that."

I trusted you. That's what he was saying and now that trust had been impacted.

A sob formed in her diaphragm and sat there as an aching lump. She'd been self-protecting.

How could she explain that she'd grown up tarred by what had been seen as her mother's failed attempt to better herself in the dirtiest, craftiest way? Sorcha could not bear to be viewed in the same light. Her pride had demanded she take all the responsibility for her actions.

"How could I tell you? You were engaged to the woman you had always planned to marry. This is what I expected." She flicked the check with her finger, sending it helicoptering off the bed onto the floor. "That's not who I am. I don't get pregnant to make money. Or to force men to marry me."

"Nevertheless, we will marry." He folded his arms.

"You don't want to marry me! You don't love me. You don't even see me as a friend! You didn't call after I left Spain. You didn't care that I was out of your life."

If she had hoped he would protest that she was wrong and he did care, she was sorely disappointed.

"I don't love Diega, either," he asserted. "Love isn't a requirement for my marriage."

"It is for mine!"

They battled it out with a silent glare for a few seconds before she tore away her gaze, flinch-

ing at what he was offering: a knockoff of the
designer marriage she had fantasized. Yes, she
had imagined marrying him, but in her vision,
love was the stitching that held it together.

"You're telling me you're not too proud to accept a onetime slice of my fortune, for the sake
of our son, but you're too proud to marry so Enrique can inherit all of it. Do you really want to
raise him in Ireland, away from his birthright?
To have him one day discover I have children
with another woman and those children are living the life he should have had?"

Sorcha sucked in a breath as though he'd
stabbed her. "You do remember," she said through
numb lips, swinging her gaze back to him.

"Remember what?" His face blanked.

"What I told you about my father that day. That
I have half siblings who inherited his wealth and
we were left with nothing."

He shook his head, irritation flashing as he
said through his teeth, "No. I remember nothing
of that day. I never will." His face spasmed into
tortured lines before he shrugged off the dark
emotion. "But I'm capable of extrapolating the
outcome if I marry another woman. She will expect her children to inherit. That's all you would
ever see." He pointed to the far side of the bed,
where the slip of paper had fallen to the floor.

All those ugly zeroes felt like bullet holes through her heart every time she looked at them.

"You just said you don't want him thinking his father didn't care enough to provide for him. I care enough to give him everything that should be his! Try telling me that you, a woman who feels as strongly about her family as you do, will do anything less than the same. How could you justify raising him alone, on a shoestring, when he could have two parents with every advantage provided for him? He deserves to inherit his *title*, Sorcha."

Okay, she hadn't mentioned that part to him, that her father's title had gone to his legitimate English son while his illegitimate Irish daughters had been turned out like squatters. It *was* horrible to think of Enrique one day feeling as she had—not only dismissed and overlooked, but also treated like trash consigned to the curb.

He doesn't love me, her heart cried. But her own upbringing had taught her that as wonderful as love was, you couldn't eat it. Should she really dismiss his attempt to offer the support she'd always wished her father had provided?

Thinking about her father and that awful realization that he'd ultimately abandoned them to their own resources brought back all her old feelings of inadequacy, the ones she couldn't put voice to because they were so lowering. Cesar really would think she was trying to trap him into marriage.

Lifting a cautioning hand, she said, "Think about that title of yours. I'm not like you. I'm working class." Gutter class, more like.

"As the mother of the heir to my title, your stock improves. Certainly with my mother." The look on his face told her he wasn't saying that to be insulting. It was a fact. Status mattered to his mother.

And that was what she was afraid of. What would happen if her background came out? It had been humiliating enough to live through it once.

"I…okay I lied," she belatedly conceded. "I only put your name on the paperwork because—"

The look on his face stopped her. The air electrified around them and she thought lightning was actually going to shoot out his eyes and incinerate her.

He gave the side of her bed a rattle of disgust, pushing away.

"*Dios*, Sorcha! You almost had me. Why would you say that?" His hand swept through the air to erase her claim.

"Because I don't want to marry you!" Another lie. She covered her face, hiding from the truth. What if she married him? Hadn't she dreamed of the chance to drill past all those tempered metals he'd hammered into a shell around his heart and find the man beneath? This was her chance.

And if she failed, he could turn out like her father, falling in love elsewhere.

"What are you really afraid of?" he asked in stern challenge. "Because I've never known you to be a coward. In fact, if anyone else was in this situation—if I was in this situation with another woman," he said, coming across to her again, words coming out faster and hotter, "you would tell me to marry the mother of my child."

She scowled. "And you would tell me there were more factors to consider and I should mind my own business."

"In this case I'm telling you you're right. Enjoy it," he snapped back.

"Look, my father didn't love his wife—"

He cut her off impatiently. "Loveless marriages can work. My parents are an excellent example."

"Ha!" It escaped her before she could hold it back.

His brows shot up.

"Do you honestly think they're happy?" she asked.

"I don't think they're unhappy. They each receive what they want from the union. In our case, you'll have a father for your child. Tell me that's not important to you. Tell me you don't wish your father had lived and stayed with your family."

That was hitting below the belt! Of course she did. She'd loved her father the way any daughter did. Losing him had been devastating. She'd been eleven, that painful age of beginning to develop and already not feeling like herself in her own body, moody and overwhelmed.

She'd also been old enough to understand what it meant that her father had two families and intelligent enough to grasp the full scope of disgrace as they were given a multitude of looks from former friends and neighbors, looks that varied from pitying to smug.

With her father in residence, he'd offered them protection from judgment. They'd lived their life as if they were his legitimate family. Without him, they were pretenders. Her mother's family, already having disowned her over the scandal of her living with a man out of wedlock, had refused to help. The entire village had distanced themselves.

Sorcha had gone as hungry as her sisters that first year, while her mother sold her jewelry and begged for any job she could get. Sorcha hadn't questioned or complained about any of it. She had comprehended all too clearly why they were living in one room and her mother was working in a hospital laundry and cried all the time.

She didn't plan to ever wind up in circumstances that dire, but that's where "love" could land you, she reminded herself. Her father's other children hadn't suffered like that. They were probably quite content, no matter how their parents had felt about each other, so why was she hesitating to give Enrique that same material security just because Cesar didn't love her?

"What would *you* get from the union?" she asked warily.

"Besides my son?" he asked facetiously. "A wife who excites me sexually." His brows went up when she gasped. "Why does that surprise you? I slept with you that day because I'd been attracted to you from the first time we met. That much I know without question. You know what else I know?"

She caught her breath, shaking her head, scenting danger as he came around to the open side of her bed.

"You wouldn't have let anything happen between us if you hadn't been suppressing the same attraction. You know what I keep thinking? You were quitting because you were jealous of Diega. Sexually. You knew that once I married, you and I would never sleep together. *I* knew that. It was bothering me. I wasn't ready to get engaged because I had promised you to myself before I went off the market."

"Do you hear how arrogant you are?" she managed to reply, heart stumbling. "You were *planning* to make me your last hurrah? That's incredibly insulting."

He ran his gaze over her in a way that drew the blanket down, exposing her to his roving eye. "I've always expected we'd be very compatible. How was it?"

"Are you serious?" She burned alive as he shoved her back into that sensual fire with a look. "*Ask Diega*. She seems to have all the details on what we did that day."

"The things I let you say to me," he muttered, touching her chin to force her to look up into his eyes.

All the emotions she used to be able to disguise in a blink flooded behind her eyes with hard pressure. She couldn't breathe.

"Of all the memories I've lost, the most maddening is not remembering what it's like to make love to you. I cannot *wait* for our do-over." He bent and covered her lips with his own, hard, but not hurtfully. He seemed to catch himself at the last second and decide whether he wanted to plunder or merely sample.

Maybe he was waiting for a rush of memory, trying to remember how their first kisses had tasted. She remembered. She wanted to protest and turn away from his kiss, but her body knew him in a primal way that made her soften in welcome. Her hand lifted to caress the stubble on his cheek, urging him to linger, playing her mouth against his in invitation.

With a gruff sound deep in his throat, he took control of the kiss and ravaged, but gently, his stubbled beard lightly abrading her skin. He claimed in a way that felt familiar, yet new. He stole, but gave back at the same time, started to pull away, then returned as if he couldn't help himself. The teasing sent flutters of arousal through her, burning her blood to the ends of her limbs, making her fingers and toes tingle. It was disconcerting to become so aroused when she was hardly in a state to make love.

It was so amazing, though. She never wanted him to stop, but he finally did with a few soft, wet bites of his teeth catching at her lips.

He drew back enough to see into her eyes. His gaze was disturbed, frustrated yet excited. Hot with desire. They were both breathing heavily.

"Seriously," he said in a quiet rasp. "How was it?"

The question felt incredibly intimate, like he was asking her to describe an experience with a stranger, yet she could see he was deeply invested in her response. He wanted details. She wanted to be flippant, self-protect and be cool and pretend he hadn't set the bar so high she had despaired before it was even over. She had known she'd never find another man to give her the same level of pleasure.

Memories flooded in, the way he'd kissed the skin he'd revealed, made her climax with barely a flexing touch between her thighs, had her wrapping her legs around his waist, then had taken his time, making love to her gently and slowly, savoring each thrust until she'd been pleading for him to drive harder and faster and deeper—

He stroked his thumb against her stinging cheek. Satisfaction relaxed his expression as he read everything he needed to know in her blush of fresh response.

"I wish I remembered that." He sounded so wistfully sincere she blushed harder and flinched in torment at the same time, raw. Feeling like the most important experience of her life was forgotten by the man who'd provided it.

And it was.

She swallowed and dropped her hand, ducking her head.

Then there was that agonizing reason *why* it had been so good. He was an aficionado of women, having dedicated himself to learning how to pleasure multitudes before her. So many.

She'd been dying on a distant level that day, wondering how she stacked up. It hadn't helped that he'd disappeared before she'd woken. She'd needed the reassurance of his approval and satisfaction. His absence had been so demoralizing she still didn't know how to deal with it. Things had worsened from there until they were here.

Frowning at the flowers Octavia had given her, Sorcha tried to imagine how she could balance the heaven and hell of being married to him. There was no question he expected her to sleep with him. What if she wasn't up to his standards? Sometimes she let herself believe that Diega had been lying when she'd said he had begged for forgiveness. She didn't want to believe she had been merely a conquest, but what else would she have been?

What if the only reason he wanted her today was because he couldn't remember that he hadn't enjoyed himself the first time?

"I'll take this back to my father and tell him you've had a better offer." He retrieved the check from the floor and folded it to tuck it in his pocket.

"Cesar—" He was such a pushy, dogged, overwhelming man.

But there was no way she could look into her son's eyes and admit that she'd had the chance to give him everything he was entitled to and turned it down. Not when she knew how it felt to receive nothing from her own father.

As for love, well, she'd long ago resigned herself to this infatuation of hers with Cesar not being returned. At least she'd be with him, not pining from afar.

"My mother is anxious to see Enrique," she said as she realized he was waiting for her to speak. "I want to go to her as soon as I'm released." *Way to be a tough negotiator, Sorcha.*

"Of course. We can marry in Ireland. One of us ought to have family present."

CHAPTER FIVE

SHE SHOULDN'T HAVE been surprised that Cesar would be so single-minded. Or so possessive. His protocols with intellectual property told their own story about the lengths he would go to ensure he would never be stolen from again.

But could he not see that if she wanted her son to have a father, that meant she expected him to *be* a father? He disappeared to Spain until she was released, asking her to text a few photos of Enrique, but showing little interest in his son or the final DNA report that proved it.

"Go ahead and forward it. My parents will want that reassurance," he said like it was a bureaucratic hoop he couldn't avoid.

"Don't *you* want to see it?" she challenged.

"If I thought you were lying, I wouldn't have upended my life to marry you. Are they releasing the two of you now?"

"Tomorrow," she replied.

He chivalrously turned up with an infant carrier, carting it out himself after interrogating the nurse about Enrique's health and schedule for immunizations, but he had yet to properly hold his son.

They went to her modest flat, where she had already been packing to give it up, planning to live with her mother through the birth and her maternity leave.

When he saw the boxes, Cesar gave her a sharp look. "Small wonder you went into labor early."

She shrugged off that comment and called her landlord to explain the situation. Cesar took over, informing the man that his assistant would have everything shipped to Spain before the lease was up and that they were leaving *today*.

Today? As much as she wanted to see her mother, Sorcha really wanted a nap.

He packed her case while she sat on the bed and nursed, then she slept on his private plane as they flew to Cork. Her customary seat greeted her like an old friend. The hostess knew how to make her tea just right and brought it without asking.

Sorcha relaxed in a way she never had in the flat she'd just vacated. She felt like she was home.

Because she was *going* home, she reasoned when she woke, groggy and thinking again that her pregnancy had been a dream. But there was

Enrique in the seat next to his father, blinking and alert, thankfully unaware his father was sending him the puzzled look he reserved for unexpected experimentation results.

They drove down the coast to her mother's village and a warm welcome.

Cesar, being a man who didn't just know how to disrobe a woman, but could outfit them effortlessly, had flown in a modiste from a Paris boutique. The bridal gown she brought only needed a few nips and tucks and the woman took care of that in her mother's lounge.

The dress wasn't something Sorcha would have chosen for herself, but it was incredibly flattering. Its empire waist disguised her recent pregnancy and its seed-pearl-encrusted bodice and off-the-shoulder straps made the most of her chest—currently her best asset. Her hair never held a curl, but the straight, golden strands looked right beneath a crown of pink rosebuds.

She looked like a Celtic goddess, strong and empowered.

Cesar spent the night at the hotel while she stayed with her family and poured out her heart, including her concerns about her marriage.

"I can't imagine any man not loving you," her sister said, squeezing her hand.

Sorcha appreciated the sentiment, but half expected to be stood up at the altar. The entire village was holding their breath to see it, she was sure, but she went through the motions of dressing for her wedding.

The morning ceremony was held in the church Sorcha had attended growing up, and was, secretly, her most cherished dream come true.

When she saw Cesar waiting at the altar for her, she felt more than relief. Pride. Joy. The sun came out long enough to splash reds and blues and greens from the stained glass windows onto the worn, golden pews and gray stone floor. Cesar had provided all the women with corsages, which, along with her elegant bouquet, perfumed the air with the scent of lilies and roses. The moment was pure and reverent.

Cesar wore a morning coat and had shaved. He hated shaving, which was why he wore stubble most of the time. He wore stubble really well, truth be told, but with his cheeks clean, his face looked narrow and sharp, his sensual mouth more pronounced.

Perhaps it was a severe mood putting that tautness in his expression, she thought, but as her sister played her down the aisle with a pretty march, he watched her with a gaze that pulled her forward. His eyes had never looked so much like white-hot metal, the green-blue giving way to silvery heat, hammered and binding.

Emotive tears came to her eyes. Was she really marrying her *boss*?

His hands were reassuringly steady as he held her trembling ones, his voice strong where hers cracked with emotion. She didn't know if that meant he was more confident in this marriage than she was, or less emotionally invested.

Financially, dear Lord, he appeared more than willing to invest. The platinum band he put on her finger was already soldered to its matching engagement ring. The stone in the one ring was a princess-cut diamond with emerald baguettes on either side, then another pair of smaller princess diamonds. The rest of the setting, like the wedding band, was alternating diamonds and square-cut emeralds.

She could hardly speak as she pushed his simple platinum band with one winking green emerald onto his swarthy hand. Hers. He belonged to her. The knowledge quivered through her like an arrow had lodged in her heart and vibrated with the impact.

Closing her two hands over his, she silently prayed, *Let him be mine.*

They received their blessing and he kissed her, keeping it chaste in this house of God, but her lips burned, making her press them together to tamp down on the tingle.

They had luncheon at the village's best hotel.

The town's seaside location meant busy summers, which sustained a few high-end establishments like this one. The rooms weren't big, but the view overlooked the beach, the decor and amenities were top-notch, and the food and service excellent.

Well, aside from the askance look she caught from a former schoolmate as the woman poured the tea.

Despite the posh atmosphere, Sorcha had to wonder what Cesar thought of the hotel and her mother's house and her birthplace. They would be sharing his suite as a family tonight and smart as she expected it to be—the suite was called The Royal for a reason—it was still far from the spacious luxury he was used to.

In the past, when Sorcha had indulged in fantasies of bringing him home to meet her family, they'd had time to visit all her favorite haunts: the beach, fudge from the sweet shop... Maybe cycle past the mansion to see how her mother's roses were doing.

She didn't know why she did that to herself, but if the weather was fine, she always went past the house where she'd grown up. It was masochistic on some level, but her father was the only member of his family who'd spent any time there. His English family had never used it. After his death, they'd sold it to an American actor, who

rarely visited. The house stood empty, which in-
furiated Sorcha all over again at being evicted.

Today the clouds were low and the sky drizzly,
so they were staying indoors. She didn't take the
gloom as a bad omen, though. The sun had made
another brief appearance as they left the church,
casting angelic rays through the clouds so the
cobblestones and brightly painted facades along
the high street glistened. In the distance, the hills
had glowed a verdant jade. The faint tang of salt
in the air was brisk and fresh, putting color in
all their cheeks. Despite her misgivings, in that
moment of leaving the church as Cesar's wife,
her future had looked brilliant.

But she wondered what Cesar was thinking
of all this. While she and her sisters talked a
mile a minute, Sorcha cast a wary glance toward
him—was he really her *husband*? Was he enjoying his conversation with the one other male in
their party, her brother-in-law, Corm?

Corm was usually very closemouthed, if en-
dearingly tolerant of his wife's family. He had
grown up around the bunch of them, since he
and her second sister had made Sorcha's niece
before either of them had finished school. They
now owned a pub and were doing well enough
with their family of four, but their early years
had been a terrible struggle.

"Football," Cesar responded when she asked him later what they'd talked about.

Of course, she thought with a private grin. Both men were fans.

"Your sister didn't stay long. Do you think—" She didn't know what she thought he should think. Her own family's scandal might have been replaced by a dozen others here in the village over the past fifteen years, but her turning up with Cesar's baby and forcing him to cancel his wedding was a fresh scandal for his.

His sister, Pia, had come with camera in hand. She was a marine biologist, who, apparently, was willing to photograph more than orca fins and sea stars. When Sorcha had thanked her for coming, she'd offered a polite if somewhat inscrutable, "Thank you for including me. The ceremony was very nice."

Had Cesar invited his entire family and only Pia had shown up?

She realized Cesar was waiting for her to finish what she was saying.

"I don't know." She shrugged self-consciously. "It didn't sound like your family was pleased by our marriage. I'm glad she came, but I was surprised to see her."

He paced restlessly, no doubt feeling claustrophobic in this narrow sitting room, if not by their shotgun wedding. "She was headed to Iceland for a symposium. It was on the way."

"Well, it was nice to see her. I'll have to send a note." She was babbling, nervous as she changed their son on the sofa, already thinking about how she would undress and share that slant-ceilinged bedroom with Cesar after they went down for dinner.

She was also feeling the pressure of this marriage, perhaps not trapped in it, but surrounded by hazards and obstacles. She was very unsure how her life would proceed.

But it was time to overcome one of her biggest concerns, she decided, as she finished zipping Enrique into his pajamas.

"Here," she said casually, scooping up the little bug and giving Cesar no choice but to take his son or drop him. He wouldn't let the baby fall, she knew that, but with that many Kelly women vying for a chance to cuddle their nephew and grandson, and a carrier with a handle making the boy feel more like a suitcase as he was transferred in and out of cars and buildings, Cesar had put off touching his son for long enough.

"What...? Why...?"

"I have to wash my hands," she said, moving into the powder room, pretending she didn't notice that the whites of his eyes were showing. "I can't leave him on the sofa. He might roll off," she called back, taking her time like she was scrubbing for surgery, glancing in the mirror to ensure her most innocent expression was firmly in place.

Enrique was just over a week old and barely keeping his eyes open for longer than thirty minutes. He wasn't going to roll anywhere for a while yet.

She came out to see Cesar wearing an uncomfortable expression. He held Enrique cradled in his two big hands, suspended in the air as though the infant was a dripping mess of sod or something equally cold and unpleasant that should be kept at a distance to avoid staining his clothes.

Her heart sank, but she reminded herself that his family wasn't like hers. His sister had come to their wedding because it was *on the way*. Had he ever held a baby in his life?

Moving across, she ignored the way he offered the boy to her and gently pressed his hands closer to his own body. "Keep him warm while I change. And watch his neck. He's holding his head up really well, but just in case. Talk to him."

"About what?" Now he held Enrique against his shoulder like he'd grabbed one too many items in the grocery store and really wished he'd picked up a handbasket.

"He's been listening to my voice for nine months and it makes him feel safe when he hears me. He needs to associate your voice with safety, too. Use Valencian. You don't want me to teach it to him. I have an accent." She headed for the bedroom.

When she glanced back, he was staring at her the way he looked when she gave him backtalk he didn't like.

"Pretend he's Corm. At least he won't contradict you over who the best goalkeeper really is."

Sorcha swung the door mostly closed and Cesar knew she was undressing behind it. *That* he was willing to help with. This…

He had held kittens as a child, when the mouser in the vineyard had had a litter, but never a human baby. He'd never even picked up a young child and this… This baby was so new and fragile, his skin so delicate, Cesar thought he'd tear him if he moved wrong.

And talk to him? He carefully eased Enrique into a more secure position in the crook of his arm and looked at the boy's unguarded expression. He hadn't needed the DNA report to believe this was his son, but he still didn't see himself in that soft, round face.

"She's crazy," he said under his breath, wanting to ignore Sorcha's ridiculous suggestion, but what she had said about Enrique finding security in the sound of his voice niggled. It's not as if he wanted the opposite, for Enrique to fear the sound of his voice, but he hadn't put together that his son would look to him for reassurance or, well, anything but basic needs and material items when he was old enough to ask for them.

What was he supposed to say? The kid was ten days old, barely able to control the wander of his gaze. He wouldn't understand a word.

Blue eyes the same shade as Sorcha's searched the ceiling with surprising alertness. So much like Sorcha's, Cesar noted with fascination. Clear and such an undeniable blue and— *Oh, hello.* Direct. Enrique's eyes found Cesar's and stuck.

Cesar found himself lifting his brows in a silent "what now?"

Enrique's tiny forehead furrowed with faint lines. His miniature brows climbed, reflecting the same query.

"Are you mocking me?" Cesar asked, astonished. A grin tugged at his mouth.

Enrique's little mouth pulled in what looked a lot like a wavering attempt at a smile.

What the hell? Cesar looked up, something rising in him that was not unlike an unexpected discovery in the lab. Sorcha was still in the bedroom. It was just him and…

There was a word…

He searched for it and found it. *Anthropomorphic.* The attribution of human qualities to an animal or object. But that's not what this was, he acknowledged as he waited with held breath for Enrique's gaze to find his again. There was a person in there, he saw, as they looked into each other's eyes. A brand-new mind trying to make sense of the world. Cesar saw beyond the lack of cognition in Enrique's gaze to the desire to get there and an unexpected thump of empathy squeezed his heart.

"I know exactly how you feel," he muttered, recalling his own awakening in the hospital to a world he didn't recognize.

He found himself touching the boy's closed fist, amused to see he was already a fighter.

Enrique opened his hand and grasped Cesar's finger in a firm grip. He might as well have closed his tiny fist around Cesar's lungs. Something happened in that moment, something uncomfortable. Cesar trusted no one, never left himself open, never gave his loyalty without a thousand tests. Yet this boy waltzed straight inside him and left a vulnerable opening behind.

At the same time, on the flip side of that vulnerability was a powerful, primal surge of protectiveness.

Cesar wasn't the biologist his sister was, but he understood on an intellectual level that parents were supposed to feel a willingness to fight to the death for their offspring. It was all part of nature's plan.

He still wasn't prepared for the rush of protective instinct that came over him, filling him with the power and imperative to ensure this boy's well-being. In that instant, he knew he could, and would, conquer anything for this boy.

Trying to ignore how shaken he was by the strange crumbling and rebuilding inside him, he lightly stroked the pad of his thumb across minuscule knuckles.

"I have your back," he promised his son, then took note of the intense stare that failed to understand the depth of what he'd just vowed. "Maybe don't wear the exact blank stare I give my own parents when I'm pretending to listen, hmm?"

Enrique was down for the night in the lounge. Cesar was glancing at the sports highlights on mute and Sorcha was staring at the bed they would share.

Actually, she glared at what had been left for her by the modiste. She had come back while they were at dinner to take the wedding gown back to Paris. She would mend any damage before she worked some kind of magic so the dress wouldn't discolor in storage.

Was this sexy peignoir her idea? Or Cesar's?

Either way, it was gorgeous, but a complete waste.

Sorcha folded her arms, staring holes into it, trying to justify starting her marriage in flannel pajama bottoms and an oversize T-shirt. But her husband had already reacted with a sideways look at what she'd worn to dinner: perfectly respectable black maternity dress pants and a white knit pullover with a cowl neck.

She heard the rattle of the remote onto a table and tensed as he came into the room. His gaze took in her disgruntled expression, then drifted to the silvery silk with blue lace poured across the fluffy white coverlet.

This was awful. She just blurted it out. "You know I can't make love, right?"

"I was there when the doctor looked at *me* and said we should wait six weeks, yes," he said drily, mostly closing the door so they could hear Enrique, but talk without disturbing him.

"Is this...?" She waved at the sexy lingerie. "Are you expecting me to do something tonight?" She was dying a death by a thousand blushes, voice thinning with how uncomfortable she was. Part of her wanted to touch him, give him pleasure. It was their wedding night, for heaven's sake, but another part...

She tried to swallow the lump in her throat.

"Do you *want* to do something?" he asked,

arms folded, rocking back on his heels. He sounded convinced that she didn't.

"I don't know," she grumbled, crossing her own arms.

She wasn't a prude, but she wasn't terribly experienced. With her mother's reputation hanging over them, then her sister's teen pregnancy, the rest of them had tried to keep a low profile. The workplace hadn't been much better. If Sorcha had wanted to be taken seriously, she had had to avoid flirting or dating coworkers. She'd had a couple of longer relationships, but her focus had always been on developing her career, not her bedroom skills.

She'd been starkly aware of the differences in their confidence levels that day in Valencia, but had thought Cesar had enjoyed himself as much as she had. Then she'd woken alone. Everything that had followed hadn't exactly reassured her that he'd been fully satisfied by her efforts.

"She asked me if she should include a nightgown. I said yes." He dismissed the conversation with a hitch of his shoulder. "It wasn't meant as a demand to be serviced." Insult underpinned his tone.

She scowled. "Don't make me feel callow."

"Callow?" he repeated.

"Green. Inexperienced. Virginal," she explained.

"Do *not* tell me you were a virgin that day." He froze, his gaze piercing hers.

"No. Of course not. I—"

"I don't want to hear it," he interrupted with a sweep of his hand.

"Excuse me?"

"I don't want to hear how many lovers you've had. This conversation ends here."

She blinked at him. "You," she said, "don't want to know how many lovers *I* have had. When you've had—"

"Not talking about it," he said, flat and decisive. "We're married now and exclusive to each other."

"Really," she said, heart fluttering with hope. "Mr. Variety Pack is willing to be abstinent for six weeks then restrict himself to *me* for the rest of his life."

He looked about to say something then changed his mind, saying after a pause, "Do *you* have a problem with that?"

"No," she said, but her voice wavered. In theory it was exactly what she wanted. In reality, she doubted it would happen.

He narrowed his eyes. "That didn't sound very convincing. *Do* you have a problem with limiting yourself to me, Sorcha?"

That was his what-do-you-mean-it-didn't-arrive-and-we're-on-the-hook-for-millions-if-we-miss-this-deadline? voice.

She set her jaw, found her spine and looked him right in the eye. "What makes you think I'll hold your interest for*ever*?"

"What makes you think you won't?" he growled.

"You left."

The aggression that had been bunching his muscles eased back a notch and his scowl went from challenge to caution. "What do you mean?"

"After we made love that day. You left." She flung a hand in the air, trying not to grow strident, but she was hurt, damn it. Scorned. "You didn't wake me. You texted me that you were seeing the woman you were supposed to marry. According to her, you said you were ashamed that you'd touched me. I can't assume you enjoyed yourself, can I? More like you couldn't wait to get away."

And now her eyes were growing damp. *Damn it.*

She looked to the curtained window. Swallowed hard. "Forget it. You're right. Let's not talk about this."

"Sorcha, I don't remember—"

"It doesn't change the fact that you did it," she said, managing to make it a steady, firm statement, but her fist knocked into the side of her thigh. "So go ahead and hate me for hiding your son, but you made me feel—"

No. She wasn't doing this.

Snatching up her flannel pants and shirt, she started for the bathroom.

"Sorcha." His voice was a whip that made her flinch and flex her back.

She stopped with her hand on the door latch.

"Look at me."

No. She kept her hand on the latch, her back to him.

He waited.

"What?" she prompted, refusing to turn.

"For what it's worth, I haven't slept with Diega."

Did that mean… She turned and tried to read beyond his begrudging expression.

"Really." She tucked the folded clothes under her elbow as she crossed her arms again. "You told me that day you wouldn't cheat on her—"

"I haven't," he groaned. "I haven't been with anyone. That's what I'm saying."

"Since me?" That couldn't be right. She was standing on solid wood flooring, but it felt like a bouncy castle.

"Since you."

She narrowed her eyes. "Are you being straight with me? She must have thought that was weird."

"She asked if everything was in working order. It is," he assured her, tone pithy. "I've checked."

For some reason she wanted to laugh. She ducked her head and pressed the back of her hand to her mouth.

He scooped up the peignoir in one motion, the silk so fine his fist easily closed over the bunched fabric. He brought it to her like a handful of Christmas tinsel. "I would prefer you wore this. If I wanted to sleep with a farm boy, I would have married one."

Cesar had expected to wake exhausted and stiff on his first morning of marriage, but had imagined it would have been from another cause, not walking a baby half the night.

Sorcha wore a wan expression as she bustled around in her efficient way, moving well enough, but she had to be just as tired.

He gave himself a mental kick, dismayed that he wasn't giving her more time to recover, but he wanted to get them to Spain. He had planned to be on his honeymoon with Diega right now, so work shouldn't be an issue, but it was. A lot of wheels had been in motion and now needed braking and reversing.

His father was refusing to step in and help him "incinerate a lifetime of planning out of sentiment" and Cesar didn't want him to. He was going to dig deep and prove this was merely a detour, not a disaster.

Still, it *was* his honeymoon and he was so sexually frustrated he could barely speak. For three long years, he'd ignored the pull Sorcha had on him. Waking to her back and butt curled into his chest and lap hadn't alleviated the ache at all. Her legs had followed the bend of his knees and the bottoms of her feet had rested on his toes, while her hair had tickled under his jaw.

She'd been cold when she'd come back after feeding Enrique so he'd pulled her into his front to warm her. He'd woken hotter than a stuffed pepper, not just from their combined body heat, but from desire.

Need.

What she'd said last night about his leaving after he'd made love to her in his office... He couldn't believe things between them had been anything less than spectacular. He hated himself for damaging her self-esteem. Men had egos in bed, but women were sensitive and physically vulnerable. As a man who had always been upfront about his inability to commit, he'd nevertheless tried to ensure his lovers felt wanted and appreciated. It didn't make sense that he would have discarded Sorcha so callously.

This damned broken brain of his.

"I'll do it," he muttered, brushing her aside

as she closed her suitcase and tried to heft it off the bed.

She flashed him a look and took the baby from him to put him in his carrier.

Had he planned to return to her with news of calling off his marriage? Delaying it? He eyed her as if she somehow knew any better than he did what had been in his mind. But despite his reluctance to marry last year, he'd always been resigned to making his life with Diega. Calling things off because he'd discovered he had a son had been difficult enough. He couldn't imagine he'd intended to break things off just because he'd had sex with Sorcha.

Diega's version, that he'd had his fill of Sorcha from one tumble in his office, didn't ring true, either. How many times had he fantasized about making love to his PA? He'd been so peeved when he woke in the hospital "engaged," and believed that he'd missed his chance with Sorcha altogether, he'd behaved like a passive-aggressive ass.

He hadn't wanted to admit last night how long he'd gone without sex. Not for any macho reasons, either. No, it just seemed too revelatory.

What he hadn't said was that Diega had made advances and he'd kissed her, but hadn't wanted to bed her. He'd been punishing her in a very puerile way for being an obstacle between him and the woman he'd still wanted, even though Sorcha had disappeared from his life.

"You don't have to get that," he told Sorcha as she picked up the envelope that had been slipped under the door in the night, thinking she shouldn't be bending like that.

"It's fine," she muttered, hair falling around her flushed face, but her expression was tight.

The *F word*. He narrowed his eyes, but the bellman had arrived to collect their cases and they went downstairs.

While he went to the exit, Sorcha crossed to the front desk.

"What are you doing?" he asked.

"Checking out." She opened her handbag.

"They have my credit card on file." He held the door and jerked his head at where their car had been pulled up. He wanted her off her feet.

Sorcha wavered briefly, glancing at the woman behind the desk as though confirming everything was in order.

The woman gave Sorcha a brow raise and a smile that was more of a sneer. "Thank you for your patronage," she said with snide sweetness. Her disparaging gaze flicked from Sorcha to the baby carrier and finally up to him.

He met the woman's cynical look and stared

her down, waiting until he was behind the wheel and pulling away to ask, "What the hell was that?"

"What was what?" Sorcha was realizing rather belatedly that her entire life had been overturned not by one male, but two. She had had months to mentally prepare for Enrique, though. She'd watched her sister adapt to motherhood and had had an idea what she would be up against.

Now she had Cesar dominating her life all over again and she wasn't sure how to handle it.

"At the desk," he elaborated.

"I thought you wanted me to pay. I always used to check us out. You paid for everything else on this trip. I thought I should pick up the room cost."

He glanced at her. "Are you serious?"

She let out her frustration in a long breath. "I don't know what you're thinking! You've been glaring at me all morning, like I wasn't moving fast enough. I feel like I'm back in my first week of work, when I couldn't make a move without getting yelled at."

A beat of silence, then he asked, "When have I ever raised my voice at you?"

"Okay, I'm afraid of hearing *that* tone. The one that suggests I'm the stupidest person who ever breathed. I don't work for you anymore, you know. I work for him." She thumbed to where Enrique's seat was strapped in behind them.

His hands massaged the wheel.

"I didn't realize that's why you were running around like it was a fire drill. I was thinking about other things, not impatient with you. I know you don't work for me. Believe me, I know. If you could come into the office and turn the new PA into half what you were, I might still have hair when I'm forty."

Sorcha looked at her nails, shaped and polished by her sister for her wedding, trying not to be smug that she was missed.

She sighed. "I liked being your assistant. You were a bear sometimes, but I knew who I was. My role was clearly defined and I had independence away from you." She lifted her gaze to the gloomy gray sky. "I realized this morning that everything is blurred now. All the decisions I make now have to be sifted through their effect on you *and* Enrique. Our relationship has to be reconfigured and I don't know what that will look like. It's bothering me."

"It is strange," he agreed. "I keep thinking I'm supposed to avoid touching you, because you're my employee. Then I remind myself you're my wife, but you're still off-limits. My libido is very confused, *guapa*."

"Being ninety percent libido, I can only assume you're extremely confused."

"There's the woman I thought twice about hiring," he said drily. "Listen. Two things. You're my wife. I will always pay and you will always expect me to."

"That's not—"

"Always. We're not negotiating. Anything I'm not present to pay for will go on the cards waiting for you in Spain."

"And if I want to earn my own money and spend it?" she challenged. Her mother's fatal error had been trusting her husband to leave her something. According to the prenup Sorcha had signed, Cesar had already arranged an income for her, but...

"We'll discuss your working when the time comes," he said in a tone that promised he would object and win. "My mother is a busy woman, Sorcha. Don't underestimate the demands of being a society wife. It is a job in itself."

She pursed her lips, agreeing that there wasn't much use arguing this issue before its time, but she had always enjoyed working. On the other hand, his mother did seem to keep busy, always organizing some charity function or other. As long as she felt as if she was making a contribution, she might be okay with letting him support her.

"You said two things," she prompted.

"Last night you said you don't want a nanny, but I want you to rethink it. I'll try to work from home while you're recovering, but I'll have to go into the office at least once a week. We'll have invitations as word gets out that I'm married—"

"Your role hasn't changed then?"

"What do you mean?"

"I thought marrying Diega was a condition to being put in charge of the family holdings. I've been worrying that marrying me had, um, impacted that?" She knotted her hands in her lap.

"My father tried that," he said dismissively. "I pointed out that whether he left me in the role of president or not—and whether my brother marries Diega or not—I still inherit the title and the family home. He's practical enough to see more work in changing course than staying it. Rico prefers research anyway and doesn't want to lead the charge. My mother sees the scandal of disinheriting an errant son greater than his marrying against her wishes, so she's resigned herself."

"That's comforting," Sorcha snorted.

He shrugged. "My father's handoff of the corporation was set back half a year by my crash so I still have a lot of work in the next two years on that. It will include some travel. If nothing else, I want you to have someone in during the day for the next few weeks so you can rest if you need to."

"I don't want our son raised by a stranger," she said, repeating what she'd told him when the topic had come up over dinner. She was heartened by his getting up with Enrique last night and his talk of working from home. Surely they could manage.

"If we lived near your mother," he said, his expression reflecting zero emotion, "and I knew you were able to leave him for an hour to get some rest, that would be different. My mother is never going to offer that sort of respite."

She supposed she ought to feel scorned, but she just felt sorry for Cesar and his siblings.

"I'll think about it," she murmured. Then she said absently, "Octavia has one." And Octavia was every bit as devoted to Lorenzo as Sorcha felt to Enrique, so maybe she shouldn't worry that hiring a nanny would break the mother-baby attachment. "I'll ask her for the name of the agency they used."

"Octavia?" Cesar prompted.

"The mother of the other boy at the hospital." Sorcha had texted her friend a selfie in her wedding dress saying, I'm getting married.

Octavia had responded with I'm going to marry my nanny. She's listening for L while I have a bath.

"Another reason for a nanny," Cesar said darkly. "We'll be in legal meetings a dozen times over the next few years."

They were quiet a few minutes, then he said, "I meant why was that woman at the hotel so nasty?"

Her heart tripped. "Pardon?"

"When we left the hotel, the woman behind the desk was very snotty. Do you know her?"

"Kind of." She probably should have been more up-front about how the Kellys were viewed by the village, but she preferred him to believe he'd married his working class secretary, not the bastard of a whore—which was what people had called her more than once.

It was so painful she hated to even reference it obliquely, but he was waiting.

"I told you how my father had a legitimate family in England?" She scratched her eyebrow. "We were quite notorious after he died. Treated like… Well, people felt Mum got what she deserved, carrying on with a married man. We were all punished. I went to school with that woman and she was letting me know she hadn't forgotten where I came from."

Sorcha looked out the window onto her beautiful country, but felt sick. With one snarky look and a handful of words, she'd been reminded what a pretender she was.

"Your mother is a very warm person. If that's where you came from, you have nothing to be ashamed of."

She smiled, touched that he would say something so nice about her mum, but he was missing the point. "Maybe I didn't get pregnant on purpose, and maybe the father married me, but I still got my husband 'that way.'"

He sent her a blistering look. "I'll cancel payment."

"Please don't. It would start something that Mum would have to finish. I'll pay it if you don't want to. It was enough for me to stand there and let her know I had the means, to be honest."

His mouth twitched and he growled, "Leave it. If you want it paid, I'll pay it, but that won't happen again."

They didn't talk any more until they were on the plane.

"Go have a proper sleep in the cabin," Cesar told her once they'd been cleared to move around. "I'll let you know if he needs you." He nodded at Enrique.

And there it was again: evidence of how things had changed. *Sleep in my bed.*

By the time they landed, the question of where their bed would be located arose.

"Does he know where we're going?" Sorcha asked, still befuddled by her heavy nap, but certain the driver had turned the wrong direction from the airport.

"We're running up the coast to look at a house. We'll stay in a hotel overnight if we decide we like it, and sign the papers in the morning."

"Out of the city?" Her heart sank. She would have preferred to stay in Ireland if he wanted her out of the way.

"Do you mind? Diega had the same reaction, but I've always wanted a vineyard and this place just came on the market."

She swung her head around. "A vineyard? Really?"

He shrugged, showing a hint of self-consciousness. "I grew up spending time with my father's vintner. It's a fascinating process. Probably the reason I went into chemistry. Jorge wasn't book-educated, so he couldn't tell me why certain reactions happened, but he was an artist for getting the results he wanted. He let me experiment. I had some successes. A few disasters," he said wryly. "I enjoyed it. Enrique might, too, when he's old enough to get his hands dirty."

She almost left it at that. If he'd still been her boss, she would have, but they were married. She took a risk. "Was? He's no longer alive? It sounds like you would steal him from your father if you could."

"He passed away four years ago. My parents

didn't tell me or I would have gone to his funeral." Cesar turned his head to look out his side window, but she saw his hand close into a fist on his thigh.

Oh, Cesar. She reached to cover his hand.

He looked down at her small hand over his for a long moment, then removed his own from under it. He gave her a faintly disdainful smile. "It's fine."

She swallowed, looking out her own window, stung. Apparently it didn't matter if she was his wife. There were still lines she wasn't allowed to cross.

The villa was stunning, sprawled across a hillside with an infinity pool that overlooked the lower bench of the vineyard and the blue-green horizon of the Mediterranean.

The interior was absent of furniture and Sorcha wasn't sure about the chartreuse in the dining room—a space that could easily seat thirty—but as they moved through the arched doorways from room to room, she mostly goggled. Ten bedrooms? Six with their own sitting rooms and baths? *Plus* a nursery with a nanny suite?

This was not her life. She subtly pinched herself as she stood in the huge master suite, slowly pivoting to take in the three walls of windows, plus the terrace overlooking the pool and sea. It didn't matter how big a bed they put in here, there would still be room to play tennis. The tub in the attached bathroom was its own lap pool.

Apparently the owners had run out of money after choosing to build a new villa rather than renovating the one that had been here for a century.

"What do you think?" Cesar asked when they returned downstairs and stood in the *third* lounge, this one an indoor-outdoor space with removable walls, a fireplace and a wet bar. "It only has a six-car garage and I don't see a space to expand it. The beach is quite a hike, but at least it's private."

Only six cars. Forty stairs to the *private* beach. Such hardship.

"Do you realize what it will take to furnish this place?" she murmured as the agent gave them a moment of privacy. Sorcha was talking about the cost, but Cesar gave her a sharp look, taking Enrique from her as she shifted the baby to her other shoulder. Their son was growing every minute and surprisingly heavy.

"I don't expect you to source everything yourself," Cesar said. "Hire a decorator so you just have to make the decisions. Paint first. That green in the dining room is hideous."

That streak of artistry in him always surprised her. He was such a man of logic and facts, but aesthetics were as important to him as function. He would have made a terrific architect.

They signed the papers the next day. Sorcha's hand trembled as she wrote her name. How did she own half of such a property? The prenup gave her their principal residence, but she felt like the biggest fraudster alive putting her name to a house like that.

Fortunately, babies had a way of narrowing one's focus down to the most immediate priorities and she didn't have time to worry about it. The next few weeks passed in a blur of meetings with decorators, interviewing nannies among staff needed for the new house, enduring fittings for a new wardrobe for herself—Cesar gave her an obscenely high budget and told her to use it— choosing baby clothes and other nursery items and occasionally being woken by her husband with "He won't settle. He must be hungry."

If she had thought it would be a time of growing closer to her husband, she was both right and wrong. They often talked as they always had. He shared work details; she gave him updates on the house. They marveled at Enrique and laughed at themselves as new parents.

Where their son was concerned, they grew very close. If Sorcha had dreamed of watching Cesar fall in love someday, her wish was granted. He stole time with Enrique every chance he could, walked him at night, changed him when he needed it, even came back to her one time with his sleeves rolled up and the front of his shirt wet, Enrique smelling fresh and damp, wearing a different outfit.

"That turned into a bath. But he's clean and dry now. And hungry."

Sometimes they watched a movie in the evenings and when she started joining him in his gym, where she walked the tread while he did his weight routine, he only asked, "Did the doctor say you're allowed?"

They slept together, often with their bodies touching. She knew he was hard every morning, but they kept their hands to themselves and their kisses tended to be pecks of greeting and departure. The domestic kind. A brief touch on her shoulder or waist, an even briefer touch of his mouth to hers on his way out the door.

Was he still getting used to the idea that he *could* kiss her? Was he showing restraint because she hadn't been cleared for sex yet? Or did he simply not want anything more from her?

If she didn't have a baby to show for it, she would think that passionate man who had seemed so driven by lust and determined to elicit the same in her had been a hot dream by a wicked mind.

So she was doubly anxious when she came

home from the doctor the day they were supposed to go to his mother's for the evening. Part of her had been wishing for weeks that they could make love and get the suspense over with. Now the moment was at hand and she found herself swallowing her tongue.

She hadn't reminded him she was seeing the doctor today. He wound up running late, arriving home as she was finishing her makeup. Leaving the ivory tower of his penthouse was enough to deal with, she decided. Aside from her doctor appointments, she had been enjoying this time of seclusion, cocooned with her baby, visiting with her family over the tablet so she didn't feel isolated.

The thought of fully assuming the title of Señora Montero publicly was intimidating the heck out of her.

Fortunately, she had Octavia. She often texted her new friend at odd hours. It wasn't unusual to find Octavia giving Lorenzo a midnight feed when she rose to nurse Enrique. Octavia was also riding the ups and downs of new motherhood and she was a terrific resource when it came to living the lifestyle to which Sorcha had socially clambered. Best of all, she made no judgment about Sorcha being a newbie to this stratosphere.

Sorcha texted her:

I need to buy some gowns. The stylist says I need at least ten. That seems excessive.

Octavia texted back:

Conservative. I bought two dozen when I married. I just bought twelve more—thanks, Lorenzo, for the ample hips and bust.

Two dozen? The gowns were four figures each!

This first event was Cesar's mother's reception for her new daughter-in-law, however. La Reina Montero was hosting a very civilized affair to introduce her eldest son's new wife to five hundred of her closest friends and relatives. In a month, La Reina would do it all again when her second son's engagement to Diega Fuentes was formally announced. One would think Señora Montero had a reduce-reuse-recycle zero-waste attitude, if not for her willingness to feed the same crowd twice.

Sorcha glanced at Cesar, glad he couldn't read her thoughts.

She had glimpsed these sorts of events from afar as his PA, and had usually been the one to arrange tuxedos to come back from the cleaners and drivers to arrive at the door. When she had asked if those sorts of duties fell to her as his wife, he'd asked, "Do you want them to?"

Much discussion had ensued about her role in organizing his private life—which harkened back to her claim that she might want an outside job again, eventually, but the truth was she was already overwhelmed. Readying their new home was a job in itself and mothering was nonstop. She liked the idea of taking charge of his personal calendar, but wasn't sure if she could handle it yet.

He wound up suggesting she needed a personal assistant, which had made her laugh outright.

"My mother has one," he'd said with a negligent shrug. Like it was a handy app you downloaded onto your tablet.

"I'm not on your mother's level," she had protested.

"You're not the Duquesa yet, but you will be. She'll judge you far more harshly for not wearing the affectations befitting your station than for acting the part out of the gate."

No pressure to be her absolute highest self tonight or anything.

They arrived earlier than the rest of the guests so they could form part of the receiving line. Sorcha felt as though invisible eyes were on her as she walked up the front steps in her heels, green-and-gold skirt caressing her thighs while she resisted the urge to tug on the strapless bodice to ensure her breasts didn't make an appearance.

She'd been to this house exactly once, in the days after Cesar's crash, when she'd brought some things from his office to his father. She'd used the service entrance and had been shown into his office for twenty minutes. She had spent nineteen of those minutes memorizing Cesar's boyhood face in a family portrait over the fireplace.

Tonight, she was a member of his family. Cesar led her without hesitation up the stairs into the private domain where he had grown up, seeking out his parents in their personal lounge. He made a point of calling them by name when he greeted them. "Sorcha, you remember my parents, Javiero and La Reina."

"Of course." Sorcha smiled. As his PA, she had used their titles when speaking to them and their greetings had been touchless. They both held her hands and kissed her cheeks today.

"Welcome." Javiero was an older version of Cesar, very handsome and still with a full head of dark hair. He stood tall in his tuxedo, jacket not yet on, and moved with economy. He never wasted a word, much like his son. Working closely with him in those first days after Cesar's crash, doing everything she could to ensure the impact to the corporation was minimized, she had thought Javiero respected and valued her.

This evening, he was inscrutable as he glanced at his sleeping grandson.

Sorcha had mostly spoken to La Reina on the telephone, ingratiating herself shamelessly in the first year of her employment. Mothers were worse than wives if you got on their bad side as a man's assistant. She figured she had one chance as his wife.

"So lovely to have you back with us," La Reina said, proving she could lie as elegantly as she could dress. "And a son. Such a delightful surprise. I've been tied up with planning this party or I would have come to see him. I thought when you'd moved into the new house would be convenient, so I could see both at once."

Tonight was not, apparently, a convenient time to view her grandson.

"I'm nursing," Sorcha said, pretending the payoff check hadn't happened. Or the generous but ironclad prenup. This was how his family did things, right? All business, purely practical, no emotion. "We couldn't leave him home."

"Oh, yes. I always thought breastfeeding sounded like such a nuisance," La Reina murmured.

Sorcha bit her tongue.

"The nanny will watch him in my suite," Cesar said. "But we won't stay the night."

"When you have him settled, join us for cocktails. Rico and Pia are here. They might be downstairs already," she added.

They left for Cesar's suite and Sorcha felt as if she could breathe again. At least it hadn't been ugly. Maybe she could get through this after all.

Thirty minutes later, she accompanied Cesar toward the stairs. He offered a hand as they began to descend and she gratefully took it, even though she kept the other on the rail. It would be just like her to go headfirst, she was so sick with nerves right now.

"Your hand is freezing," he said, closing his warm one more tightly over hers.

"I'm terrified," she muttered. "What are people going to say?"

"Congratulations," he replied. "What else can they say?"

"I suppose," she mumbled, and told herself to quit frowning, but couldn't shake her worry. "Are you sure I look all right?"

He was exceptionally handsome in his tuxedo, wearing it like old jeans. He'd shaved and wore the bored expression of a man who'd done this too many times to count.

"I told you before we left that you look beautiful, but Enrique started crying. You might not have heard me."

"No, I did. I just—" Didn't believe it. She'd seen him with his lovers in the past. He'd always been so attentive and indulgent, performing fore-play with light fingers on a woman's skin and nuzzles of his lips against her cheek.

She was his wife and while his compliment had sounded sincere, he'd also seemed stiff when he'd said it. Standoffish. He wasn't flirty and affectionate with *her*.

They reached the bottom of the stairs and she let go of his hand, turned to face him and made herself confront her worst fear. She had always felt attractive, if wary of her own allure, but the changes of pregnancy had her confidence faltering.

"Be honest. Is the baby weight turning you off? Because I'm trying to drop it as fast as I can, but it's hard."

"Sorcha." He looked genuinely shocked and confused. "What gave you the idea…? Even if you were still out to here—" he stuck his hand in the air at his middle "—it wouldn't matter. You always look flawless. You're the most naturally beautiful woman I know."

"I'm sorry. I'm just really nervous and—" She was such an idiot. She shouldn't have started this here, now, but this party felt like the official beginning of their marriage and she wouldn't relax until she at least knew… "I went to the doctor today. She said we could, um…" She looked around. "You know," she said in an undertone.

"If we use, um," she swallowed and mouthed, *condoms*.

He stared.

She felt as though she grew transparent, skin thinning with heat, clothes incinerating until they flaked off her body in papery curls and she stood naked before him. She had just handed him the power to accept or reject her, leaving her self-worth hanging in the balance. She wished he would—

"You tell me that now? Here?"

"Where else—"

"The shower? An hour ago?" An avid light fired his gaze and his hand wrapped firmly around her arm. He steered her down the hall, but rather than taking her toward the main area of the house, he tugged her past the office she'd seen last time, then into a billiards room.

She scuffled along, fearful she'd be pulled off her heels. "Cesar, you're scaring me."

"I wait three damned years, then you disappear for eight months. I *marry* you and still have to wait six weeks…"

He pushed through a frosted door into a humid solarium. The scents of oranges and earth, lilies and herbs, were so pungent, it was almost overwhelming. The room was dark, lit only by the lights surrounding the tents erected outside. The glow filtered through small panes of glass, most of the light kept out by the abundance of greenery growing upward and dangling from hooks.

It was enchanting, but… "You want to, um, here—?"

"I want," he growled, pulling her into his arms and pressing a hot, openmouthed kiss against her neck. His hand slid low, taking firm possession of her bottom to press her into the hardness of his unquestionable erection.

"Oh!" she cried, clutching at his shoulders for balance.

"I have been wanting and waiting and you finally tell me I can have you, but that I have to wait a little longer? I never took you for cruel, Sorcha." His breath moved the tiny hairs along the edges of her updo, tickling and stimulating her sensitive nape, sending shivery waves of pleasure through her whole body. Gooseflesh rose on her arms.

She had wondered what had happened to the unabashedly sexual playboy she used to work for and here he was, flicking his tongue against her earlobe before he caught it in his teeth. He was moving his hands all over her waist and hips, sliding the silk against her skin, learning the shape of her thighs and buttocks. It was a disconcertingly familiar touch, kind of shocking in its level of ownership, but it sent tingles of anticipation and excitement through her. It felt really good to be touched. By him. So greedily.

Heat suffused her as she arched her neck and found herself turning her face, seeking his mouth with her own.

A sound tore out of him and he covered her lips with his own, full and knowledgeable. The sweet, occasionally lingering kisses of the past six weeks were gone. This was raw, undeniable passion. His tongue pierced unapologetically and searched for hers. Her abdomen contracted with excitement.

A deeper moan escaped her and she crowded closer to him, loins flooding with a hot ache, dampening with excitement. They stood there barely moving but for caressing each other in erotic pulses of their bodies against each other, mouths mimicking the thrust and reception they both craved.

With a little sob, she tore her lips from his, panting as she said, "I didn't bring any condoms with me. I left them in the table by the bed. Do you have one?"

He drew back and even in the shadowed light, she could tell he was glaring.

"You had one that day," she protested. "I thought it was something you always carry, like a credit card."

"No," he growled. "I don't have one and I'm

not about to consummate our marriage on a potting table in my parents' garden shed."

"Save it for our anniversary?" she suggested.

He looked to the glass panes of the ceiling, shaking his head. His hands were still flexing on her. "This is going to be a very hard, *hard* evening to get through."

She ducked her head against his chest, sheepishly delighted. The evening ahead began to feel more like a date.

"Thank you," she murmured. "I feel pretty now."

"You are more than pretty. You're radiant," he said, sounding as if he meant it. They exchanged another kiss that promised a "to be continued."

A moment later, drunk with arousal, she let him lead her back into the billiards room. They would make love later. The knowledge whispered and sang inside her, like a delicious secret. Like Christmas was coming.

He followed her into the powder room and stood next to her in front of the mirror, swiping her color off his mouth, then expertly refolding his kerchief to hide the stain before replacing it in his jacket pocket.

She eyed the maneuver.

"I won't ask how many women you've dragged into that solarium," she said as she reapplied fresh lipstick to her tingling mouth. She really didn't want to know.

"I've never fooled around with anyone in there during a party," he said. "Too much chance of running into my brother."

CHAPTER SIX

BUOYED BY HER dalliance with Cesar, Sorcha *felt*
radiant. And optimistic.

He made her feel magnetic, looking at her constantly, hand not just resting on her back, but
thumb caressing the edge of her gown where her
skin was exposed.

Even the thought of having to face down Diega
didn't dent her confidence. She felt rather pro-
tected, flanked by Cesar on one side and Rico
on the other. Like one of the fold. Rico was cast
from the same mold as his older brother and father, dark and handsome, tall and well built, capable of flirting and flattering, but with the same
distance from emotional attachments as the rest
of them.

"Did Cesar tell you I offered to marry you?"
Rico had asked while bringing her a cocktail
earlier.

"No," she had said, stunned. "Why on earth
would you do that?" She'd met him several times

while working for Cesar, but had rarely exchanged more than appointment details or an offer to fetch him coffee. With Cesar firmly holding her interest from the first, she'd never seen Rico as anything but one of her boss's high-level associates, never a romantic prospect.

"You're smart, pleasant and attractive. It was a practical solution. Enrique would have had our name and a proper share in the family fortunes. Diega would have had the title she wanted," Rico said with a diffident shrug. "You could have relayed the offer," he added, speaking to Cesar now. "She might have preferred a lower profile. Did you think of that?"

He wasn't joking.

Neither was Cesar when he said a clear and flinty "No."

"It's moot now," their father said, and the men began discussing the technical properties of new alloy.

"Tell me about the house," La Reina prompted Sorcha.

She gave a short rundown, carefully filtering everything she said, determined to leave the right impression. "Cesar said I should hire an assistant, but I've been interviewing staff for the house and the idea of going through the process for yet one more position right now... I can't face it. What are your thoughts? Do I need one?"

She mentally laughed at how pretentious she sounded.

"I'll have mine do the preliminary screening. You're right, it's too much when you've just had a baby. You have just the one nanny?"

Their nanny was the most underworked caregiver in continental Europe, considering how enamored Sorcha and Cesar were of their son, but Sorcha only said, "For now."

The small talk wrapped up and they now stood in the foyer of the family mansion, greeting all of Spain as far as Sorcha could estimate.

She might not have been raised in high society, but her father had been titled, educated at Cambridge and a member of the House of Lords. She knew what good manners looked like and had learned early to adopt his posh accent for job interviews, especially in London. Cesar had been taken aback the first time he'd overheard her talking to her mother, falling into their broad Irish accent as she did. Already firmly entrenched as his PA, she had had a moment of insecurity as she danced around explaining that she was actually peasant stock, not the snobby aristocrat she mimicked.

Tonight she was pretending to be exactly that, determined to make Cesar and his family proud to call her a member of their family. At least not ashamed.

It was all going well until, quite suddenly, the Marques de los Jardines de Las Salinas was in front of her, congratulating her on her marriage. He was Diega's father. Then her mother was in front of her, also offering a distant smile.

"Querido," Diega said to Cesar, her smile wide and avaricious as she arrived with her parents. She paused to kiss both his cheeks. "I brought an old friend of yours. I hope you don't mind. As I said to your mother when I called, perhaps we can make a match for Pia." She sent a moue down the line, winking at Cesar's sister before bringing her gaze back to catch at Sorcha's. Her smile hardened. "Cesar was at school with him," Diega explained. "Thomas Shelby. The Duke of Tenderhurst. Do you know him?"

Sorcha's heart stopped. The Duke of— *Her half brother?*

"Tom," Cesar was saying. "Nice to see you."

Sorcha couldn't bring herself to look. Her gaze locked to Diega's triumphant one as Diega moved along to Rico.

Sorcha told herself to breathe, but she was turning to stone, like a spell had been cast, filling her insides with gravel and earth and hardening agents. Clay. Gummy, suffocating sludge.

"Meet my wife, Sorcha," Cesar said, oblivious. Her half brother showed not a hint of recognition as he took her limp hand and claimed it was nice to meet her.

His smile faltered until she found a stiff one, then he shook her hand and said something about how happy he was for her and Cesar. He wished them a long life and moved along the line.

Get through this, Sorcha told herself, grappling for composure.

The worst part was, he looked just like her da.

Cesar wouldn't call himself intuitive, but spending time with a baby developed a few skills for reading a mood. He knew what the dismayed precursor to an emotional meltdown looked like and Sorcha teetered for a millisecond on that bubble, obviously knocked off-kilter by Diega's arrival.

After their stolen moment of passion earlier, he was in a state of sustained tension not unlike the final moments before climax, when his control wanted to unravel. He'd been thinking they were both standing in the fire of sexual awareness, burning with anticipation, but she was no longer with him.

What could he say about Diega being here? He'd forewarned her. He'd chosen Sorcha and his son over her. That ought to count for something.

Sorcha recovered quickly, making him almost doubt he'd seen anything. She now held a smile on her face, greeting people and exchanging pleasantries, but he could tell she wasn't herself. And her behavior was odd because she had disguised her falter well. He was surprised with himself for noticing the change in her. He hadn't realized how attuned he'd become to her.

What she looked like, he realized with a hard shock, was like one of them. The natural warmth he took for granted, in the same way he expected her blond hair or blue eyes, was extinguished. It had been replaced by a facade of forced good manners.

They were finally able to leave the door and move into the crowd that had spilled out to the lawn and open-sided tents. The orchestra paused so his father could make a toast, welcoming Sorcha into the family.

She smiled, looked as radiant as Cesar had called her earlier, but ethereal. Insubstantial. Her eyes were shiny and the strain behind her expression suggested she was quietly miserable.

And that misery felt like a knee to the groin. He was pleased to introduce her as his wife. Proud. Despite the costs to his family and the impact on their relationship with Diega's, he had concluded his son was worth it. Once they lived properly as husband and wife, he would no doubt be more than satisfied.

Was she not pleased to call him her husband? They started the dancing and she was a mannequin in his arms, not the receptive woman from earlier, but a stick figure that held him off.

He reflexively turned himself inward. Aloofness was his comfort zone, but it was difficult to maintain when the promise of physical intimacy had been bending the barbed wire he kept in a perimeter around his inner self.

"I should check on Enrique," she said as the song finished.

He realized she was trembling and tightened his hands on her, trying to still the odd vibrations rolling off her.

"What's wrong?" he asked, surprised to sense he was being rejected—which was an extraordinary enough circumstance without the heavy dose of reacting to it with a feeling of injury that weighted his insides.

"Nothing." Her smile was such a blatant lie, it was a slap across the face. "Excuse me."

He did not follow anyone and beg for affection. He let her go.

The nanny looked up from where she was reading a book in the sitting room. Enrique was sleeping in the cot next to her.

"I have a headache," Sorcha choked with a weak smile and pointed to the bedroom, then closed the door behind her.

Sinking onto the foot of the bed, she wrapped

her arms across her middle and told herself not to cry.

"Oh, God," she whispered, more racked with fear and pain than she had been while in labor. *Oh, God, oh, God, oh, God.* She rocked, trying to ease the agony ripping upward like a tear from the very center of her being into her heart, rending and leaving jagged edges as it climbed to score her throat.

She was going to lose him. This time, when she told him about her father, there would be no sidestepping for a prettier angle. They might have grown closer than they'd ever been over their few weeks of marriage, but she hadn't found the right way to explain what a pariah she really was.

Was Diega enjoying telling him? Sorcha hadn't been able to wait and watch him realize what he'd married. Had she honestly imagined it would never come out?

She would have to face his disdain now.

Cesar had gone to school with him. Tom. Her husband's *friend* was part of the evil, awful— He didn't even know who she was! He had never even cared enough to look up a photo or find out his half sisters' names.

Why would he? They were *trash*.

Don't cry, she begged herself, pushing her bent knuckles against her trembling lips.

The door clicked and her husband stood in the

opening for a long moment, observing her. His scowl might have edged toward concern, but her eyes blurred and she couldn't tell.

She rose, wobbling in her shoes as she moved to the box of tissues. Plucking several from the holder, she dabbed her face, trying to stem the pressure beneath her eyes, but tears leaked onto the crumpled tissues, staining them with mascara and eye shadow.

"I did tell you," she said, like it counted for anything that she'd confessed to being illegitimate. That was a far cry from whatever was being whispered about her downstairs. Tom was one of them and she already knew how quickly she would be exiled as *not*.

She was right back to that moment of walking across the schoolyard, when everyone had stared. The headmistress at the door had given her a cold look and someone had whispered, "Bastard."

Her sister had held her hand in a sweaty grip while Sorcha had sought out her best friend, Molly. She'd seen Molly every single day since they'd both been in nappies, but Molly had only mumbled, "Mum says I shouldn't be friends with you anymore."

Sorcha had survived it and had stopped caring that people had refused to serve them, but the fact Cesar was going to react the same way had her stomach churning.

"Maybe I should have foreseen this could happen," she said, voice traveling through razor blades all the way up from her lungs. "You're both titled. I don't know why I'm shocked you're acquainted, but I honestly didn't mean to—" She sniffed.

She hadn't meant to bring her shame into his mother's house and attach it to their son. How had she thought this wouldn't happen?

"I told you she would be here. Resign yourself to seeing her, Sorcha. She and Rico—"

"It's not her," she choked, shaking her head. Diega was a catalyst. She was the spark, Tom was the fuse, but Sorcha's mum taking up with a married man was the keg of dynamite that was causing her life to explode.

Gripping her own elbows, Sorcha looked to the ceiling, trying to stem the tears.

At what point would they be finished paying for her mother's mistake in loving the wrong man?

"Sorcha, I haven't seen you like this except for that time with your niece. Has something happened with your family?"

She choked again, this time on hysterical laughter. "Yes. Ha."

Her voice started to waver and she dug her fingernails into her skin, using the physical pain to overcome the crevasse widening down the middle of her heart.

"I told you my father married for money? To save his estate? He didn't love his wife. Couldn't stand her. Once his children went to boarding school, he spent all his time in Ireland, only going back to England when his son and daughter were home. You must have noticed the house on the hill in my village? That's where we lived with him."

"You lived there?" He sounded surprised.

Of course he was. It was a showpiece. A far cry from the tiny row house where her mother took in travelers to help pay the mortgage.

"Da spent a lot of money fixing it up. It made him popular in the village, hiring local builders and such. Mum was his maid. He fell in love, no surprise. She was twenty to his thirty-eight. When she became pregnant with me, she moved into the house proper. We lived like a real family, if you overlooked the fact he had another family in England. Most people pretended to, since their livelihoods depended on his keeping the house open."

She risked a glance at him, dabbing under her nose as she did.

He was listening, probably wondering where she was going.

"He promised Mum the house, but that didn't happen. It belonged to his 'real' family. When he died, they sent a lawyer, told us the property was part of the titled holdings and evicted us."

"How old were you?" He narrowed his eyes, as if trying to recall if she'd told him this before. "There were four of you, by then? And your mother?"

She shrugged and nodded. "I was almost twelve."

"That's a long time to be a man's pretend wife. Your mother didn't contest it?"

"How? She sold her jewelry to buy groceries. She wasn't even allowed to keep the car he'd given her. The whole village turned their backs on us because she'd been living in sin. The only people who were kind to us were the staff we'd lived with at the house. They helped her find a room over a carriage house. We shared it for two years until I was able to start working and help with rent."

She blew her nose.

He was completely unreadable, arms folded, only the penetrating glacier-blue of his eyes moving as he searched her expression, filing this new information into his mental database.

"All five of us in one room with a single hot plate and no refrigerator or even a proper bath, just a toilet and a sink with a curtain. No one at school would talk to us. Mum had to ride the bus into the next village to work and even then it was only washing dishes and doing laundry for a hospital. Even waiting tables was impossible. People were horrid to the bunch of us for years."

"Like that woman at the hotel," he ventured. "Why didn't you move?"

"To where? *With what money?*" She came to the heart of her story. "I tried to tell you in the hospital that I wasn't in your class. I should have tried harder, obviously, but I really hate talking about it." She pinched the bridge of her nose, stemming the pressure underscoring her eyes. "It's so humiliating. But I should have been honest. Pretending I've risen above it makes me the trash they called me. Now it's all going to come out downstairs, when Diega tells everyone Thomas Shelby is my half brother."

CHAPTER SEVEN

CESAR WASN'T USED to being angry. Not at this level. If he'd thrown tantrums as a toddler, they'd been reasoned out of him by the time he had made permanent memories of his earliest self. Yes, he had moments of frustration and irritation. He had a low tolerance for incompetence, disliked people who played politics and was never happy if his brother happened to win against him at anything.

The most incensed he'd been as an adult had been waking to the infuriating loss of a week and the long recovery his injuries demanded. Still, he'd kept that to merely a lousy mood that had clung stubbornly right up until, hell, he supposed it had finally started to dissipate sometime between holding his son for the first time and necking with Sorcha in the solarium.

But even as miserable as he'd been stuck in the hospital, staring down a marriage he didn't want, he'd kept his cool.

Not tonight.

Sorcha worked hard. He knew few people who worked as hard as she did with as few complaints. Her work ethic was only surpassed by the quality of her work, which was why he'd always respected her.

He'd seen how modestly her family lived, too. He had known pretty much from the start that she sent money home and knew she was still squeezing funds for them from her savings. He had padded the account he'd set up for her to ensure she could keep helping out at home without denting anyone's pride. He admired her even more since their marriage, now that he'd seen how far she'd come from her disadvantaged beginning to the position she'd held with him.

And she was *kind*. Warm and cheerful and never one to strike back at rudeness with equal harshness. He liked to keep the pressure on. Not everyone responded well to that. Aside from the occasional dark look, she'd always sucked up his demands with a smile.

Sorcha was that rare creature: a good, solid, hardworking person.

To see her devastated like that, eyes hollow, calling herself *trash*…

Cesar wound his way through the crowd until he spotted Diega, then reminded himself to keep his hands by his sides, rather than forcibly re-move her from the home she so coveted.

She was holding court with his parents and Rico, her smile smug.

He leaned in from behind and spoke through his teeth next to her ear. "Leave. Now. You know why."

Rico sent him a startled glance. "Mind your manners, big brother."

Diega paled, turned her head and looked past him for Sorcha before her mouth tilted into a disdainful smile. "I don't know what she told you—"

"Just as I will never know exactly what I said to you, when I saw you before I crashed. Was I really proposing, Diega? Was I?"

She held his gaze, but her eye twitched. It might have been the confrontation. He'd never come at anyone with this much animosity, but it might have been a tell. He scented a lie.

"Cesar." Rico brought up the back of one firm hand to press it against Cesar's chest, obviously reading his dangerous mood.

But he wouldn't soil himself by touching that viper.

"Our family does not attack itself," he told Diega. "You won't be invited to join it. Leave. Quietly. Don't make a scene. You will regret it."

"Cesar!" his mother protested in a shocked whisper.

"She leaves or my wife and I do, Mother. Take your pick."

His mother was speechless for about half a second. "An explanation would be nice!"

"Diega gave up 'nice' months ago, when she hired someone to follow Sorcha. Didn't you? You weren't surprised she was pregnant. You knew and didn't tell me. I've often wondered how I went through that rail. Did you slip me something, trying to keep me at your house?"

Rico swore under his breath and his hand dropped from Cesar's chest.

"No!" Diega gasped. "That's a repulsive accusation!"

Cesar wanted to believe that was earnest horror, but bringing Tom here set a high bar on how ugly she played. "You just took advantage of the situation once I'd crashed?"

"I will leave," she said with a lift of her chin. "I won't stand here to be insulted." She scanned the crowd.

"See her into her car," he said to his brother, barely staying inside his skin, he was so livid. "I'll find Tom."

They arrived at his penthouse late. It hadn't been a long drive from his parents', but Sorcha had fallen asleep in the car, sliding on the leather seat so she wound up slumped into Cesar's shoulder.

Disconcerted by his stiff, silent air of threadbare tolerance, she settled Enrique for the night, then moved to the bedroom to begin undressing.

She really didn't know how to take his mood. He was sipping a whiskey, standing at the door to the small terrace off the master bedroom.

"Mother expected Diega to help her organize a fund-raiser for May. She mentioned as we were leaving that it might be better if we host it at the new house, take the focus off the fact that Rico and Diega won't be marrying after all."

"Um, okay." She removed her earrings. He'd given her the pretty yellow sapphires before they left the house. She picked at the catch on the matching bracelet, trying to open the clasp. "I'll call her tomorrow to ask the details?"

"Give it a few days. She'll need to regroup after tonight."

"I'm sorry," she said, voice wispy. It wasn't just the lateness of the hour. She was worn thin from hours of tension.

"Here." He came across to remove the bracelet, poured it into her hand, then indicated she should turn so he could open her necklace.

His touch was gentle, but the vibes radiating off him were dangerous.

She'd never seen him like this and didn't know

how to interpret it. After saying, "I'll be right back," he'd disappeared from the bedroom at his parents' then returned thirty minutes later.

"Tom was shocked," he'd stated. "He said his grandfather on his mother's side held the purse strings and had a solicitor who was equally ruthless. He'll review how everything was handled. I said my lawyers will be in touch for a full examination of the will and probate, too. He and Diega are gone now. Will you fix your makeup and come downstairs? Mother would appreciate if we pretend nothing has happened."

It had taken her several heartbeats to comprehend what he'd said. Then she'd numbly done what he asked. With a fresh mask of makeup in place, she'd circulated on her husband's arm. He'd been quiet, not unlike the contained businessman she'd worked for. The only difference was that he was in physical contact with her the entire time. Whether it was holding her hand, setting a heavy hand against her back, or drawing her arm through his, he kept her very close to his side.

But it hadn't been the sort of solicitous affection she craved. It had been protective, but intimidating. Possessive.

Catching her necklace before it slid into her cleavage, feeling her dress loosen as he lowered the zip, she kept her eyes on the floor and said huskily, "I thought it was enough that you knew we were poor and my mother wasn't married. I should have told you the rest. I'm sorry. I know you're disappointed. It's only because your respect means so much to me that I…"

She had cried enough earlier. She wouldn't let another sob release now.

"I didn't want to lose your good opinion," she continued in a strained voice. "And I know I have. What do you want me to do? I can't leave without Enrique. I can't."

Her heart twisted inside her chest. She started to move away, but a warm hand closed over her upper arm, strong and firm, keeping her from stepping away. His fingers began searching her hair to release the pins that held it up.

"You are not trash. Do not ever let me hear you call yourself that again."

His voice was so at odds with his light touch in her hair, she froze. She told herself it was the pull of pins tugging tiny strands of hair as he gently dragged them free that made her eyes sting. She tried to be indignant that he did this so proficiently because he'd removed pins and jewelry and evening gowns from countless women.

But when her hair fell, soft and tickling around her bare shoulders, he hooked his forearm across her collarbone and drew her back against his front, big chest expanding, breath hissing as he settled his jaw against her temple.

It was a quiet, tender moment that she couldn't help but savor.

"I'm furious," he admitted in a low growl. "Furious that it happened and furious that Diega, someone our family trusted, deliberately tried to humiliate you. I want you so much I can hardly breathe and I'm afraid to touch you because I'm in a mood I don't know how to control." His thumb stroked her skin below her shoulder while his forearm sat heavy across her front, pinning her before him.

He was hard. Not just aroused against her bottom, but tense all over.

She touched the sleeve of his jacket and felt his rigidity through the layers.

"I've never had anyone defend me," she said, turning her face into the fabric of his jacket, letting herself sink against him in gratitude. "Thank you."

She tried to turn, but he resisted, easily keeping her facing forward, then released a ragged curse and pivoted her into him. Her arms went around him as though he was the one in need of comfort when she felt so exposed and fragile she could hardly bear it.

He wrapped strong arms around her, one hand

dragging through her hair to pull her head back so he could scrape his teeth against her throat.

"Stop me now if you're having second thoughts," he said against her skin, tongue painting a line to her nape.

"I'm not," she gasped, transfixed by a kind of paralysis as he conquered her with the simple act of opening his mouth against her neck.

It was basic animal dominance and submission. Her nape was sensitive and his strength disciplined. She folded as any living creature would, succumbing to that strength, trust blooming when he could harm her yet didn't. She was rewarded by tiny exquisite shivers of pleasure that raised goose bumps down her arms.

He drew back and the look in his eyes belonged to a marauder claiming spoils. His gaze didn't waver as he pushed down her loosened dress.

She gasped, started to catch at the bodice, but he stopped her, holding her hands in the air as the dress slithered into a puddle around her feet. He kept her hands up as he slowly and thoroughly studied what he'd revealed. Pale skin, heavy breasts that had been supported by the bodice and were bare now. Hips plump enough to give definition to a waistline she'd only begun to start finding again. Thighs that—

All thought stopped as he put her wrists together in one of his hands and dropped his free hand to slide a finger beneath the top of her underwear, slowly working them down. The back of his knuckle grazed her folds.

She jerked, catching her breath.

His gaze came up, holding hers as he deliberately brushed against her again while easing the stripe of green lace so it was a tight line across the tops of her thighs.

"Cesar," she protested. Hot pressure flooded into her loins, making her ache.

"How close are you?" he asked in gruff Valencian, turning his hand so the pad of his fingertip lightly traced her seam, gently parting and sliding easily in the evidence of exactly how aroused she was.

She flinched with sensitivity, biting her lip and closing her eyes against how intimate this was.

"Look at me," he said in a rasp. "Open your eyes or I'll stop."

She opened her eyes to slits, begging him with her gaze to give her some privacy as she dealt with what he was doing to her. She tried to pull her hands free, but he didn't let her.

"I have wanted and wanted and wanted," he said, tracing low then covering her with his hand in a warm blanket of heat so she throbbed with reaction, breath stuttering.

He held her in his hot palm and it was too flagrant, yet not nearly enough. Not after those first teasing caresses.

"Do you want me? This?"

She nodded shakily.

"Show me."

She didn't know what he meant, but pressed into his hand, lost in the passion that turned his eyes a vivid green. He held his hand steady for her undulations. Flutters of excitement rose through her belly and trembled in her thighs.

He praised her in Valencian, telling her she was beautiful, that what she was doing was nice. Exciting. "You're so wet. I always knew you would respond to a firm hand in the bedroom," he said, looking at where she was rocking against his palm.

She sobbed, thinking that he'd said something like that the first time, but he pressed a finger inside her and her mind blanked.

"Keep moving," he coaxed. "Do you like that?" His thumb swept and a lightning bolt of intense pleasure contracted in her abdomen, making her shudder. "You do."

"I can't stand," she gasped.

"I won't let you fall. I'm trying to be gentle. Is this too rough?"

"No. It's not…"

"Not enough? Move with me. Show me how you want it."

She did. She stood there and let him watch her and pleasure her until her thighs were shaking and her muscles contracted and cries of release broke from her parted lips.

He gathered her in as her knees weakened, damp hand slipping free to catch behind her thighs as he picked her up. She quivered in his arms, clinging, stunned as he carried her to the bed.

He peeled her underwear away as he left her on the mattress, then stood looking at her.

She threw her arm over her eyes, mortified at how uninhibited she'd just been.

"Oh, *corazón*, if you're feeling shy after that, you are in for some shocks. I have a lot of fantasies to fulfill."

"You're not supposed to have dirty thoughts about your employees." She peeked from beneath her arm in time to see a wolfish grin flash.

He stood at the side of the bed to drop away his cummerbund, then tore his shirt open before he yanked it from his pants and off his golden shoulders. Muscled arms wrenched out of sleeves and one cuff link hit something across the room with a *ping*.

"I don't have dirty thoughts about all of them. Just you. I mentally bent you across my desk daily," he confessed casually.

Her jaw slackened. "That's...*bad*!"

He jerked open his pants, efficient as he stripped.

Last time… She stopped thinking about last time. It was too much like a dream. This time felt like the first time all over again, even more profound.

If possible, he was even more perfect than he had been then. He was flawless, from the rope-like muscles across his chest to his neatly muscled arms. An arrow of hair dissected his perfectly delineated abs and a pale tan line accented the crease at the tops of his long, taut thighs.

And then there was the long, thick, darkly flushed organ that barely moved as he skimmed his shorts away and leaned toward the night table.

"I never acted on those thoughts," he said. "My favorite was the blue skirt that was just a little too short for the office." He brought a box out of the drawer. "You always wore it with that prim little shirt with the round collar that had a button that strained just a little bit, right here." He pointed to the spot on his breastbone between his nipples. "I wanted to rip open that shirt and push that skirt up to your waist so badly."

"I'm beginning to wonder if I did all the work and you were just sitting there thinking about sex."

"I multitask."

Didn't he? In one motion he tore open a blue packet and applied the condom while arousing her with a few naughty remarks and the blaze of sexual hunger in his gaze as he visually traversed her nude form.

She wanted to show some modesty and shield herself, but there was a brazen part of her that enjoyed his obvious hunger. She thought about the way he'd taken her apart and wanted to have the same effect on him.

Giving a little writhe on the coverlet, she watched for reaction, surprised when he reached out and stilled her knee. His gaze flashed into hers and she thought, *Oh.*

"What's wrong?" she asked, voice a breathy taunt. "You told me that day that I needed a man who would take control because I have too much of it. Do you still think that?"

His expression shuttered as he covered her with his hot body, hard legs moving between hers to push them apart and make space for himself. His hips lowered against hers, firm shaft pressing against tender flesh.

She shivered with anticipation.

"Say my name," he growled as he held her head in two hands.

"Why?" she asked, letting her fingers trace the bulging muscles of his arms where he caged her.

"Because I want you to."

She smoothed the sole of her foot on his leg. The movement caused a little rock of friction where his shaft rested against her.

He let more of his weight settle on her hips, stilling her tease. His stare warned her to comply.

She smiled. "I don't work for you anymore. I don't have to listen to you."

"You're my wife. You belong to me."

"Do I?" There was something wrong with her that she responded to that possessiveness. But he wasn't a man who collected things for the sake of it. He was spare about the things he accumulated, but he insisted on the best. To be counted among what he valued meant something.

"You do," he assured her, shifting so he could palm her breast. Lowering his head, he breathed hotly across the tip.

Her nipple tightened so fast it hurt.

"Cesar," she gasped.

"Good girl," he said, giving her a lusty, superior smirk.

She scraped her nails against his shoulder, but he only shaped and massaged her breast. "I liked watching you come against my hand," he said gruffly. "It used to drive me crazy that you would rather take a memo than let me make love to you." His thumb flicked across her taut nipple and she felt it as a sharp pull in her abdomen and a flood of wet heat between her legs. "I admire control, but not when it prevents me from having what I want."

"Who wants to give up a career for a one-night stand?" she asked with a hitch of her breath that held bitterness. "I needed my job more than I needed an orgasm."

"It was a very good orgasm, wasn't it?" He nipped her chin then looked down at where she was rocking her hips against him. "You already want another one."

"Don't *you*? I thought you had been waiting *so long*," she said, goading him.

His nostrils flared and he slid his hand down between them, exploring and making her breath catch again, finding her ready for him and smiling faintly. He guided himself to her entrance and pressed.

The penetration stung. Not bad, but enough for her to press her hand against his chest to still him.

"Hurt?" A panicked look came into his eyes.

"A little, but it's okay." She shifted, relaxing and inviting him to continue.

He held himself very still, swearing as he glared at her. "You're going to kill me, Sorcha," he warned.

"But what a way to go, hmm?" A smile trembled on her lips and she let her calf slither across his tense buttocks, encouraging him to drive deeper.

He groaned, ducked his head to cover her mouth with his and slid home, hard and fast.

He shuddered. She let out a little sob that was both pleasure and pain.

He held still again, letting her get used to him. They kissed and she wriggled under him, trying to incite him, but he only stopped her long, drugging kisses.

"Cesar," she gasped when he let her, feeling urgent. It wasn't just sexual frustration. It was months of wanting to feel him moving in her again. It was being convinced a few hours ago that she would lose him and having him rise to protect her. She loved him. In this moment, she loved him so deeply she wanted to pour her whole self into him. She wanted him to mark her, claim her, use her up.

"Gently, *tesoro*. I don't want to hurt you," he said, peeling her fingers from his hair to lock them over her head in a firm grip. Then he kissed her again, deeply and passionately, just this side of ravaging. And he stroked the side of her breast, caressing around and under, dancing his fingers across her nipple so she whimpered into his mouth with pleasure.

Her secret terror was that he would only want her this once. She ought to be savoring this moment, letting him take it slow, but she was hungry and greedy and eager.

"Please," she gasped, turning from his kiss. "I need you to make love to me." Her eyes glittered with emotion. Her breaths came in shaken pants. Her entire body trembled.

He released her hands and drew back. She dug her nails into his shoulder blades, reeling under the sudden stimulation and his incredibly possessive look. He returned with an air of luxury, each thrust and withdrawal becoming a reinforcement of his right to make love to her.

She wrapped her arms tighter around him, moaning in glory, caressing his buttocks, feeling them tighten as he pushed deep, making her scalp tingle and her loins clasp at his intrusion, eager to hold onto the delicious sensations.

"You're mine," he growled, asserting himself with the full weight of his hips. "Say it."

"You're mine," she said, scraping her nails on his butt.

He growled and kissed her, hard, thrusting with more purpose, one hand tangled in her hair so she couldn't move her head without feeling a pull. They both made noises of struggle and exquisite agony, enjoying the build. She thrilled as he held her on the cusp of release, both of them tense and sweaty, barely able to breathe as they kissed and clashed their hips together and reveled in the pleasure they gave each other.

When the crisis hit, she gave herself up to it, to him.

He broke away to let out a jagged cry as he climaxed, big body racked as he tried not to crush her with his strength, hips locked to hers, pulsing deep inside her.

"Mine," he said, head hanging so his damp forehead met her collarbone. "You're mine."

CHAPTER EIGHT

HE HAD HIS ANSWER, Cesar thought dimly as he worked up the strength to roll off his wife, reach for a tissue and discard the condom.

Prior to his accident he had gone to Diega, if not to cancel his wedding, then to at least put it off. There was no way he'd left Sorcha because he had notched his bedpost and was done with her. Once was *not* enough. That, what he'd just had with her, was a type of insanity.

Granted he was a possessive man and her talk of leaving him and taking Enrique had provoked him when he was already in protective mode because of Diega's actions. He'd set out to *prove* she was his tonight, but even if the first time had been only half as cataclysmic as this, it was still the best sex he'd ever experienced.

What had that day been like? It bothered him that she had memories of it and he didn't. It felt as if she had a secret. He didn't like it.

But if he had left while she was sleeping that

day, it was because he wouldn't have been able to wake her and still walk away.

The smoke alarm could go off right now—it should be ringing like a five-alarm fire as it was—and he would be loath to climb from this bed.

And when she was looking at him like that? Mouth swollen, eyelids puffy, the orgasm flush still pinking her cheeks and that quest for reassurance turning her expression so very solemn.

No man could resist rolling back against her. He cradled the side of her face and kissed her, an inexplicable urgency bunching the muscles of his back as he did. He wanted to take her again, now, maximize the time they had—

He lifted his head and looked down at her, startled by a thought and so pleased he couldn't help but blanket her with his weight and tug her under him, asserting his ownership with the pinning of his thigh across hers, but with a foreign kind of tenderness rolling through him. Excitement that was not fleeting, but carried deep, long-term gratification.

"I always thought there would be an expiration date on our lovemaking," he said, hearing the husky satisfaction that was warming him as the truth sank in. "I was okay with waiting to make love to you because I knew I'd have to give you up afterward, but I don't. I can have you for the rest of our lives."

"At least until you're too old to get it up."

"Learn to bite that tongue, *preciosa*," he warned with a glint in his eye. "Or I'll do it for you."

"I don't know what I'd do without you, Octavia, I really don't," Sorcha told her friend over the tablet. She had always thought she'd done the hard part of organizing an event when she had sourced all the options, but making the final decisions was the more stressful task. "If I had to ask my mother-in-law for advice, she'd think me completely incompetent."

"You're not at all— *Grazie*," Octavia said to someone off-screen, then showed Sorcha the cup of espresso she'd been handed. "I'm sending you some of these beans. One of Sandro's contacts in South America got us onto it and they're incredible."

She was curled up in the corner of a settee and both of them were enjoying a rare conversation without at least one of them nursing or soothing a baby. Both boys had finally cut their bottom front teeth and were napping soundly.

"I thought the first time we entertained, it would be a few of Cesar's business partners, not hundreds of strangers. His parents will be the only people I know. I wish you could come so I'd have one friend, at least!"

"Of course I can, if you want me to."

"Are you serious? Yes, please! I would love that!"

She'd opened up to Octavia a lot since they'd met, but her friend had no real idea how out of her depth Sorcha was. She couldn't talk to her mother about how insecure she felt as Señora Montero, either. It was like complaining about winning the lottery. And her mum wanted to believe Sorcha was living happily ever after.

She was, to some extent. They were settled in their new home and Cesar had fallen into working a couple of long days at the office in the first half of the week, then working from home the rest. She and Enrique had accompanied him for a brief business trip to France and he'd delegated another to Rico so he could stay home.

Cesar took Enrique when he walked the vineyard on Saturday mornings, usually leaving her in bed, dozing off his lovemaking. They made love constantly. Inventively.

So she told herself to quit being so damned greedy. A girl like her couldn't ask for more. Wasn't it enough that she had a man who told her she was beautiful when she was still wearing her robe and didn't even have her evening gown on yet?

* * *

"Can you zip me?" she asked the night of the gala, moving across to where he stood fastening his cuff links.

Her gown was a simple, strapless black with a ruched waist that gathered on her hip, disguising those last few pounds she was still fighting to lose. A scalloped, off-the-shoulder lace overlay of three-quarter sleeves would lend it a Spanish flair and her hair was pulled to one side in a rope of straight gold that had fallen behind her left shoulder.

Cesar's warm fingertips smoothed her hair to the front, baring her back to him, making her shiver.

"Like that?" he murmured, stroking her exposed spine down the length of the open zipper. "I can't stop thinking about your mouth around me the other night."

"Cesar," she gasped, clutching at where her heart almost leaped out of her chest. "Why do you always talk about it?"

"Because it turns you on," he said, tone heavy with smug amusement. He continued to caress her nape and set a kiss where her neck met her shoulder. "Doesn't it?" he demanded against her skin.

She was blushing, flushed with pleasure at

knowing he enjoyed their lovemaking as much as she did.

He lifted his head and something cool and smooth and surprisingly heavy slid across her upper chest.

He clipped the necklace into place, then zipped her dress before touching her shoulder to turn her.

"Oh! I didn't know I'd be wearing it." She moved so she could see herself in the mirror. The pendant on the thick platinum chain was a teardrop-shaped blue sapphire set in a splash of platinum rays accented with glittering diamonds. Cesar had arranged with the jeweler to have it included as part of her silent auction fund-raiser. "It's so beautiful."

"On you, very," he agreed, appearing behind her and smoothing her hair back behind her shoulder again. "And that clinches it."

"Clinches what?" She met his gaze in the mirror.

"I'll make the final bid. There are earrings to match." He nodded at the open velvet box on the side table.

She was only touching the edges of the stone, not wanting so much as a fingerprint to dull its sparkle, but she looked up at him with a kind of admonishment.

"I don't expect this, you know." She'd already

picked up on the great pride his mother took in showing off things her husband purchased for her, but Sorcha didn't see how Javiero's buying a red convertible for his wife translated into anything but a conversation starter over lunch.

"The part where you married me and come home to us is the part that matters," Sorcha told Cesar.

"I know," he said, something like tenderness softening his hard features. His caress on her jaw was light and sweet. "I've never understood that about you."

"That I would value a person over a thing?"

"That you don't expect anything for the amount of yourself that you give up," he explained.

"What does that mean? That if I could afford the right item, I could have more of you?" She kept her tone a light tease, reminding herself that his world had never been like hers, where all she and her family had *had* was love, but his remark made it sound as if he would never love her. That shook her.

"What more do you need?" he asked with a light frown, as if he couldn't imagine what he was failing to provide.

Oh, Cesar.

She was glad to have the distraction of the party to take her mind off the fact he couldn't see she wanted his heart.

* * *

Cesar's world had always been one where status mattered. He didn't buy in to it the way his mother did, but he still felt his youthful failure as more than just a financial disaster. It was his greatest embarrassment that he'd let personal feelings get the better of him, lowered his guard and left himself open to becoming a mark.

His parents' disappointment had been nothing compared to his disgust with himself.

Sleeping with Sorcha, getting her pregnant, crashing and calling off his wedding… That was more weak, mortal behavior where he'd allowed passion and other emotions to govern him. Even his conversation with her earlier, over the necklace, was niggling at him, making him discontent.

He was reserved for a reason, damn it. He couldn't afford to be emotionally vulnerable.

So his mother's approval of Sorcha's party meant very little to him one way or another. Sorcha, however, felt things deeply. He knew that, which was what he'd been getting at earlier. She shouldn't put so much of herself on the line for things like this party.

She was *so* invested in its success.

While he might not trust easily, he'd been more than confident she would pull off a stellar event. Could she see now that she was showcasing their home beautifully and everyone was enjoying themselves?

See? he wanted to say to his parents. Marrying Sorcha had made sense. She was smart, made a charming hostess, had sophisticated tastes...

She didn't see all that she was, of course. She was the most humble person he'd ever encountered. While tuxedoes and evening gowns mingled in the sparkling lights of the garden, and everyone conversed happily in and out of the silent auction tent, his wife stood beside him holding her breath, pretending she wasn't straining her ears, waiting for his mother to pronounce judgment.

Finally his mother nodded to indicate an Italian couple. "They seem interesting. His mother is marrying the Count of Valdavia. Did you know that, Cesar? He was very generous with his bids in the auction, too. You might break my record," she added in a chiding tone aimed at Sorcha that nevertheless held a note of admiration.

If his mother was bested, it had better be in a way that put a larger plaque on a wall with their name in grander letters.

"I only had the chance to say hello when the Ferrantes arrived. Do you mind if I go speak to them now?" Sorcha asked him, loosening her grip on his arm.

"I'll come," he said, excusing them from his

parents before his mother asked how Sorcha knew them. He had never mentioned how he'd come to learn Sorcha was in hospital with his baby and the hospital had kept a lid on the scandal as well.

Cesar might have refused to let Sorcha invite the Ferrantes given how they met, but he understood all too well how one could trust by mistake. Diega's recent betrayal was still casting a shadow.

He wouldn't have brought up the baby switch with Alessandro Ferrante, either, but the moment Sorcha left with Octavia to check on the boys, Ferrante apologized for his cousin's perfidy. He wore such an air of self-recrimination, Cesar understood the man felt these sorts of failures as deeply as he did.

As furious as Cesar was that the man's cousin had nearly stolen Enrique from him, he had read the reports. Ferrante wasn't letting sentiment keep him from encouraging the law to do their job.

A shred of something he suspected was Sorcha's influence, put a positive spin on it, prompting him to confide, "I wouldn't know I had a son if it hadn't happened. Don't apologize. I'm grateful."

Ferrante nodded, seeming to relax a little. It clearly wasn't a surprise to him that Cesar hadn't known about his son. That told him Sorcha had confided that detail to Octavia.

He suffered a moment of exposure, realizing his private life wasn't as private as he had assumed. He took a fresh measure of Ferrante, thinking it might behoove him to know him better if their wives were gossiping.

"The ladies have plans to lounge by the pool tomorrow, but I'll be spending the morning in our vineyard. I understand you have a private label as well? Would you like to join me? Our vintner would love to pick your brain on your methods."

Ferrante took a moment to consider. "Sounds more interesting than working from my hotel room. What time?"

It turned into a more pleasant day than Cesar expected. Sandro Ferrante might not have his depth of scientific education, but he was very sharp, brought a knowledge of the process that was almost second nature and had an excellent palette. They wound up joining the women at the pool for the afternoon, sampling bottles from the existing stores, discussing improvements and debating modern versus traditional methods of winemaking.

Cesar even held the other man's son when Sandro moved inside to return a call he couldn't ignore. Octavia was in the pool and Lorenzo woke abruptly and started to cry.

Cesar couldn't ignore him while his mother dried off and put on her wrap.

He picked up the tyke and the boy felt oddly similar to his own sturdy son, his little hand resting on Cesar's shoulder in an endearing way.

He stopped crying and stared at Cesar, trying to decide what he thought of a stranger holding him. He didn't even have tears on his cheeks. He wasn't upset, just letting the world know he was awake.

Cesar couldn't help grinning at that.

The boy returned a crooked smile so quick and beaming, it made Cesar chuckle.

Octavia took him and sat to nurse so he turned away, catching his wife watching him from the water. "I might have gone home with him. Isn't that something to imagine?"

And he wouldn't have known. He would be married to Diega, living in the city. Working nonstop to keep his mind off the turn his life had taken.

As opposed to now? When work was something he resented a little because it took him away from his family? When had that happened?

Did his wife realize how much of himself he did give her?

Sandro came back at that moment and said they'd have to head back to the hotel soon, so he could take care of some work details while

Lorenzo had his siesta, but he invited them for dinner. They ended the night with promises to visit the Ferrantes in Italy at the first opportunity.

"That was such a nice day," Sorcha said after returning from dinner, pleasantly relaxed as she readied for bed. She loved her sisters, but was beginning to feel like she had a fourth one in Octavia. "Thank you for being so gracious with them."

"They're easy to be around," Cesar said, pulling off his tie and unbuttoning his shirt. "But you told them I didn't know about your pregnancy, didn't you? That's not like you."

Her conscience pinched and she finished removing her earrings before she answered. "I told Octavia when we were still in hospital. It was a stressful time, waiting for the results so they would believe us. You were so angry. She was my only friend. I honestly didn't look at it as talking about you. I was confiding something about myself."

He eyed her in a way that made her heart sink.

"You're angry."

"No," he said firmly. "I would prefer you didn't share our private business with others in future, but no. I'm angry that I can't remember that day, Sorcha. My entire life took a hard right and I will never fully understand why."

She went to him, half expecting rejection because he was not a man who appreciated compassion, but she was a woman who offered it freely when she could.

His expression remained remote as she threaded her arms around him, but he rested his arm across her shoulders, holding her loosely while that distracted frown stayed on his face. Then he looked down at her.

"Tell me again what happened."

She did, stumbling slightly when she got to the part about him claiming not to subscribe to love, thinking about the moment yesterday over the necklace. Then she repeated his reasons for feeling duty-bound to marry Diega and blushed as she got to the bit where they had bantered about whether he would cancel his engagement if she withdrew her notice.

If you let me have you, I might.

"And then?" he prompted.

"And then we made love," she told him.

"How?"

"What do you mean, 'how'?" She started to draw back. "The normal way."

His arm hardened, keeping her right where she was. "Missionary? Clothes pushed aside or completely naked? I can't believe I leaped on you. I'd been thinking about it a lot. I must have taken my time? Start with the kiss and tell me exactly what happened."

"No. Cesar," she chided, shoving at his hard, flat stomach, but he only shifted her so they were face-to-face, hips-to-hips. He was becoming aroused.

So was she, not that she wanted to admit it, but she couldn't talk about making love with him without thinking about how it felt and that just made her want to do it.

"I'm serious," he said. "I kissed you and then what? Where in the office were we?"

"The sofa."

He backed them to the bed and sat her next to him.

"How did I kiss you? Show me."

"We're not doing this," she said, face so hot it hurt.

"We are," he assured her, leaning forward to brush his mouth against hers. "Show me."

She was just annoyed enough to do it. She came up on a knee so she was taller than he was, put her hand behind his head the way he'd held hers and kissed him with firm purpose.

A jolt went through him at her aggression, but he wasn't the type to submit. He adjusted their position and took control of the kiss, as commanding as he'd been that day, consuming her as if it hadn't been just this morning when they'd last made love.

When she was pliant and leaning into him, he lifted his head. "Then what?"

"You pulled me into your lap and we kept kissing."

He did, hand stroking her bare thigh where the skirt of her cocktail dress dropped away in loose pleats. "What were you wearing?"

"Pants. We'd been on the bridge that morning and it was windy. I didn't want to risk a skirt."

"The black pair that shows off your ass really well?"

"Cesar!"

"They do." He shrugged. "On top?"

"The sheer green over the light green cami."

"Nice. You never wore a bra with that."

"Because the cami had one built in."

"I could still see your nipples when they were hard. Did I tear it?"

"No!"

"Did I suck your nipples through it? I always wanted to."

Wicked, sexy flutters contracted her abdomen.

"I did," he said with a lusty narrowing of his gaze before he looked down at the lined bodice of her indigo dress. One strong arm went behind her back, arching her up as his head went down.

"Cesar!" She grappled for his shoulders, bottom firmly imprinted with the thickness of his prodding erection as he opened his mouth on her breast and bit lightly at her nipple through the fabric.

She writhed as he aroused her very deliberately, just aggressive enough to produce sharp sensations through the material.

"Did you do that then?" he asked, looking at where she rubbed her thighs together in restless friction, trying to ease the ache between.

She swallowed. "Maybe."

"Did I open your zipper and help you find relief?"

She shook her head, wondering where she got the nerve to talk about this, but the weeks of lovemaking they'd already enjoyed had created this safe place between them, where they could be raw and brazen and intimate. She could see he was enjoying this in his own wicked, kinky way and she wanted him to. Being the only one with the memory of that day was hard for her, too.

So she ignored the shyness that accosted her and guided his hand to her mound over her skirt. "You rubbed me through my pants and..." Her voice broke as he settled his palm into place with comfortable ownership while memory of what had happened reduced her voice to a whisper. "We kept kissing and I kind of…" She bit her lip, blushing hard, but she knew he would like it. "I had been thinking about making love with you for a long time, too."

"You came?"

She nodded.

His nostrils flared and his arms flexed, pressing her hard into his lap, as if he needed the pressure of her bottom against his straining flesh to keep from losing control just from hearing she'd lost hers.

"I was really embarrassed, but you said it was hot." She searched his expression. His cheekbones were flushed and carved into sharp relief, like his scalp was tight.

"So hot," he assured her, caressing her with purpose. "Can you do it again?"

"You get so mad at me for the things I say to you, but look what you do to me." He must have felt her trembling. "I don't want to play games, Cesar. I want you to make love to me." She kissed his neck.

He bared his teeth. "I like your back talk as much as you like my teasing. When did I undress you? I must have been impatient. I am now." He smoothed his hand down her leg, then back up her bare thigh under her skirt.

"We did this..." She touched her foot to the floor long enough to press herself onto the bed and bring him over her.

He rode her lightly through their clothes as she breathily confided, "You told me if I hadn't reacted like that, you might have been able to stop at a kiss, but—" She kissed him. "We couldn't seem to stop."

"I don't want to," he growled, kissing her passionately, hand under her skirt again so he could caress her hip and the back of her thigh as she hooked her leg around him. Curling his fingers in her underwear, he said, "These must have come off. That's all I can think about."

She pressed her lips together and nodded.

He lifted to skim them away and glanced into her eyes. "Then?"

She hesitated too long, not wanting to lie, but not wanting to say.

A light of understanding dawned. He grinned wolfishly. "Isn't that interesting? It's exactly what I'm dying to do right now. Please don't be modest, *corazón*. I want you to ask me for what you enjoy. Did you like it?" He was lifting her skirt to her waist, exposing her naked thighs to the cool air.

"Yes," she admitted, mortified. "But I didn't— I was self-conscious and you were really turned on so you stopped before I— Oh!" The first dab of his tongue stole her voice.

"I think we can do better this time," he said, breath hot on her mound, and he did do better, making her gasp, then moan, then cry out his name.

She was sweaty and wrung out when he stood and threw off his clothes. He dragged at her dress and bra, and said, "You could help," as he stripped her.

"I really can't," she murmured, practically purring as she smoothed her arms across the covers. It was all she could to do lift her knees to bracket his hips as he settled his nudity over her. "But we *were* completely naked except for this—"

She touched his hard flesh covered by a condom and guided him.

He entered her, sliding deep in one thrust.

"And it was just like this. I love feeling you inside me," she told him on a gasp, pushing her hands into his hair, arching to his thrust.

"I love being here," he said in a low rumble, opening his mouth on her shoulder as he began to withdraw and thrust. "I can't get enough of you."

She ran her hands down his damp back, enjoying the flex of his muscles as he moved slowly and deliberately, watching to ensure she liked it.

"How many?" he asked.

"We don't have to break any records." She grinned at his arrogance.

"Tell me."

"Two."

"I can definitely do better than that."

CHAPTER NINE

THE MINUTE CESAR arrived home, he sought out his wife, finding her in the sitting room talking to her mother on the tablet.

She didn't roll her eyes when he ruefully showed her the teething ring he'd found in his jacket midmorning, the one he'd obviously pocketed the last time he wore this suit and that she'd been searching for high and low ever since.

In fact, she looked quite distressed, lifting a searching gaze as he entered. Her mother's voice, so similar in tone to Sorcha's, but with that heavier accent, was saying, "I didn't want to tell your sisters until I'd spoken to you and found out if it's true."

Cesar was pulled up short by Sorcha's expression, heart taking an uncomfortable kick. He hated seeing her upset.

"What's wrong?" he asked.

"I'm not sure. Mum says a lawyer from London wants to meet her to discuss her settlement proceedings against the Shelby estate for the house and other income she should have received as a beneficiary in Da's will. Would that be your lawyer? Is it just a preliminary thing?"

"That was weeks ago. Is he only calling you now, Angela? That's not acceptable," Cesar affirmed, moving into the screen so his mother-in-law could see him, hands instinctively going to Sorcha's shoulders in a comforting caress.

"Hello, Cesar," Sorcha's mum said with her dazzled smile. "No, he called ages ago and that was your Mr. Barrow again, on the telephone from London today. He said he would forward you a full report if I wanted him to. The Shelby family has admitted provisions were made for us and we're in a position to sue for damages above what was owed in the first place. He wants to meet to discuss it and I... Well, when it seems too good to be true, it usually is."

"In this case, I expect you're seeing justice at work," Cesar assured her, pleased on her behalf. "I'll check with Barrow, but my advice would be to hear what he has to say. I'd bring Sorcha so we could sit in, but I'm leaving first thing in the morning for Dubai. This presentation has been in the works for nearly a year and can't be put off."

He had suggested Sorcha invite her mother or sisters to stay while he was gone, not liking to leave her alone. None had been able to get away and she hadn't wanted to come with him. His schedule was full and the heat and local customs would keep her in the hotel most of the time so she hadn't seen the point.

"He said he'd come Monday, but I'll see if he can wait until you can be here," Angela said, hand to her forehead as though dizzied. "Oh, Sorcha, do you realize if you hadn't fallen in love with your boss, none of this would be happening?"

Beneath his light hands, her shoulders stiffened and a strangled noise was quickly muffled in her throat.

Sorcha offered a brisk promise to be in touch about their travel arrangements and ended the call, ducking away from his touch. She would have walked out of the room if Cesar hadn't caught her arm.

A kind of shock held him. She *loved* him?

Women had said the words to him in the past, but he'd always dismissed them. It wasn't something he had ever wanted to hear or could say with conviction himself. Frankly, he'd never believed any of those women and told himself not to put much stock in it now.

But there was something very compelling about being granted entry into the tight circle of people Sorcha held closest to her heart.

"Sorcha?" he asked, gripped by anticipatory tension. "Do you?"

She skimmed her gaze down, biceps tense in his light grip. "Do I what?"

He touched her chin with his free hand, insisting she look at him. Her eyes were their darkest blue, the pupils large and deep, her mouth tremulous. Her vulnerability was hard to witness, but he had to know. With a gentle caress against her cheek that he meant as reassurance, he asked quietly, "Do you love me?"

The word felt like a phrase in a foreign language he was trying for the first time.

Her brow pulled in a flinch and her eyes grew shinier. Her mouth opened, then she closed it again, as if she couldn't decide how to respond.

He dropped his hands, startled by a deep stab of disappointment. "I didn't think you'd lie to your mother about something like that."

"I didn't," she said quickly, folding her arms. "I mean. Yes, I do, um…" She cleared her throat. "Love you," she said with a little thrust of her jaw, brow a line of determination as she dragged an air of confidence around her.

He'd seen her don this look a thousand times when the pressure was high and now knew it was her defense mechanism, something she'd learned to wear against those who'd been hard on her after her father's death.

She shouldn't feel a need for it with him. Laughter rose in him, the kind fueled by soaring joy. It was alien, yet powerful, like a ferocious storm he ought to fear, yet a primal part of him reveled in it.

"Why haven't you said?" he asked, bemused.

She finally met his gaze, searching so deep, he went on guard. Angst crept into her expression.

"Do *you* love *me*?" she asked.

He mentally took a long step backward. Here was the issue with deep feelings. They turned quiet words into explosives that could go off if they weren't handled very carefully.

Love had never been on his radar. A psychologist would accuse him of taking all those lovers to counter the absence of affection in his youth, but he would argue that he had a healthy sex drive. He'd learned early to take pride in his accomplishments and let his self-esteem hinge on his opinion of himself, no one else's. He didn't yearn for acceptance or fulfillment. He was utterly secure.

Even with his son, he didn't nurture to earn the unconditional adoration Enrique showed him. He met his son's needs because it filled him with deep, personal satisfaction to see the boy content. Did he love his son? He suspected that yes, he did, but he hadn't framed it in so many words to himself.

What he felt toward Enrique was simple and instinctive, but his regard for Sorcha was more complex. He was in the most intimate relationship he'd ever had, but was this love? He was too honest a man to blurt out such a statement without being absolutely sure.

How could he be sure, though? His scientific mind wanted points on a graph. A series of tests and results. Hard data.

"You know I'm not wired for it," he said cautiously.

Sorcha told herself he wasn't saying that to be cruel, that she had always known this about him, but his deflection still felt like a knife to the chest.

She was facing down his lost memory of Valencia all over again, but in a higher, more acute octave. She loved him. She had begun to believe he had feelings for her, but he didn't. Not on the level she was at. Everything she thought they shared was actually only in her mind, her heart. There was nothing on his side but sexual attraction, respect perhaps and a strong sense of responsibility.

"That's why I haven't said." She hated that her voice wavered. "I should check Enrique."

He didn't let her go. "It doesn't mean we can't be happy. You're happy, aren't you?"

She wanted to claim she was and walk away, just to end this painful moment, but she shook her head.

"I've been telling myself I should be," she said, staring blindly toward the hall. "You're the one who told me I shouldn't take on another dependent just to feel loved. When I married you, I told myself it was better to have a husband who provided for me, than one who loved me and left me to fend for myself, like Da did to Mum. I thought it was unrealistic to expect both love *and* material support, but it's not. Da did make provisions for us. He loved us *and* wanted to take care of us."

She swallowed, still taking this news in. All her mixed, resentful feelings toward her father fell away and love, wistful love, was left. It was freeing, yet painful, making her ashamed that she'd doubted him.

And it cast her marriage in a dark light. She had settled for support, which wasn't a bad thing, especially when she'd had hope for love.

But her husband wasn't wired that way.

Hope was gone.

The walls of their gorgeous house came into focus. The furniture she'd chosen with such care, wanting to create a home for them, suddenly seemed very superficial. A placebo for the environment of love she'd really been seeking.

"I'm going to check flights," she said. "I'd like to see Mum."

"Not wait for me?" He tightened his hand on her arm, not hurting, but she could feel his tension.

"I need to be with the people who *do* love me."

"Sorcha…" The way he said her name was a jagged score against her heart, making her want to seek comfort from the very man who was destroying her.

"If you loved me, you'd understand how painful this is," she said, shaking off his touch.

He flinched. "You're not taking a commercial flight," he said stiffly. "The jet can take you this evening and come back for me and Rico. I'll make some calls."

Cesar was still brooding days later, standing in the suite he was sharing with Rico, staring out at the green-blue expanse of the Persian Gulf.

He hated that Sorcha wasn't in their home, but told himself it was good that she was with her family. She had looked so miserable, he hadn't known what else to do but give her what she wanted and send her to the people who always made her smile.

He hadn't made her smile.

Damn it, that was the problem with emotions.

They left you susceptible. He didn't *want* to hurt her. She's the one who'd allowed him to.

"Why aren't you changing?" Rico asked, coming into the sitting room with damp hair, buttoning a fresh shirt. He swore. "We're not going to a club, are we?"

"*We* aren't, no."

Rico hung his hands on his hips. "I never expected to see you mope because you weren't home with your wife."

"She's at her mother's and I'm not moping."

"Just because the rest of us are incapable of showing a shred of humanity doesn't mean you can't admit to affection for your wife. We can all tell you think your son is the most important thing you ever made."

"He is," Cesar said, turning to confront his brother.

Rico hitched his shoulder. "Not the way we were raised to think, but Sorcha would agree. Why do you think I offered to marry her? I knew she'd be warmer with her children than Mother was with us. And Diega? Can you imagine her with a child? She'd eat it. Be honest, you knocked up Sorcha to get out of that marriage, didn't you?"

"I don't remember that day," he reminded coldly. He had a very nice replacement memory, but his original motivations remained a mystery.

Rico snorted, rocking back on his heels. "How about all the days leading up to it?" he challenged. "Remember those? Because you were always going to sleep with her. I knew that the first time I met her, when you looked at me with a promise to kill if I didn't stop flirting with her. If your interest in Sorcha was only physical, why put off having her? You were keeping her around because you liked her. What are you afraid of if you admit you care for her? That she'll steal company secrets?"

Cesar fisted his hands in his pockets. "No. I trust her implicitly."

"Ah, it's me you don't trust," Rico said in a tone of enlightenment. "You don't want to admit you have a weakness where she's concerned."

Not even to himself, Cesar thought grimly, but couldn't deny it. He was missing more than his son. He wanted his wife. He wanted to taste her skin, feel her against him in bed, hear her laugh. He wanted to watch her hands move as she told him a story.

He wanted to know how things were going with her mum. He was worried that she was being treated badly by the locals and hated that he wasn't there to protect her.

He wanted to hold her, suspecting he might have made her cry. He wanted to reassure her it would be all right, but would it?

How could he make things right if he *didn't* love her? How would he even know what love was? Blood didn't come from a stone. If the raw material wasn't present, you couldn't extract it. What they had was chemistry—

He tipped his head back as realization frothed up in him as quickly as bicarbonate foamed in vinegar.

One element could bond to another, forming something that wasn't present before. He knew that as conclusively as he knew his lungs took in oxygen molecules that could attach to hydrogen and become the water that made up seventy percent of his physical body.

He and Sorcha certainly generated enough *heat* to support a chemical reaction.

Hell, love wasn't a substance anyway. It wasn't something you found and weighed. It acted like an energy, one with enormous power. Sorcha's love wasn't sitting within him, taking up space. It was radiating through him, like light, accelerating his own emotions.

He quite suddenly *urgently* wanted to be with her. His need to feel her and smell her was magnified, expanding like a supernova, wanting to swallow her into him with the understanding they'd both be stronger for the bonding.

And apparently love had the ability to slow time, because the two days before he'd be home to see her suddenly stretched like an eternity. Would she even be there? A black hole opened inside him as he understood what he'd done to her that day.

If she wasn't there waiting for him, it meant that he'd killed her love.

If you did love me, you'd understand how painful this is.

He did understand. He felt sick at deflecting what had been the greatest possible gift she could give him.

Moving to his phone, he quickly texted, asking if she was on her way home.

Tom wants to meet us. I'm staying for now.

Cesar's heart stuttered in his chest.

She'd left him once before, but he wasn't comatose in a hospital this time. He wasn't going to let it happen again.

Everything, from the moment her mother had spilled Sorcha's heart to being home again, where her mum said things like, "See? Falling in love with your boss isn't a disaster," was heart-wrenching.

Cesar didn't love her. Sorcha told herself to be content with what she had. They were closer than they'd ever been.

But this was as far as they would go. She had to come to terms with the death of hope.

Thankfully she had her mother's settlement package to distract her.

The biggest news had been that the mansion on the hill was being procured from the actor who'd bought it. Their old home would soon belong to her mother.

They had all debated at length about whether Mum should move into it. In the end they decided it didn't matter how anyone in the village reacted. They had all learned to live with judgment long ago. If that was the home her mother loved, she ought to live there if she wanted to.

That set the groundwork for her mother to hire a manager to keep her existing house open for lodgers and its modest income.

She kept saying that with that income, she didn't need anything more than the settlement she'd been entitled to in the first place.

Sorcha, having worked in the cutthroat business world, understood there was a time for kindness and a time when being nice got you nothing. After all they'd endured, she was not going to let her mother be talked out of one euro less than what she deserved. She had a vision of Tom Shelby swanning in and reminding her mum so much of the man she had loved that he'd soon have her signing away her claim to everything, including the house. No way was Sorcha leaving until all the *t*'s were crossed and *i*'s dotted.

Corm, bless him, suggested they meet at the pub so they felt as though they had home-turf advantage when Tom arrived. They were all quite nervous and it turned out to be a surprisingly amiable afternoon.

Tom opened with what sounded like a heartfelt apology. He explained that his mother was still alive, but in a home with dementia. He'd been a minor when their father died and his grandfather had had power of attorney. The grandfather had orchestrated the fraud, his signature was on all the papers prepared by a now dead lawyer. Tom was leaving it to a court-appointed authority to determine a fair settlement.

He was being as decent as he could be in the circumstances and Sorcha had to allow that she might have judged him too quickly in Spain. His remorse and desire to mend fences seemed very real.

"My being here is personal. I wanted to meet you properly," he said, explaining that his— their—sister was working in South America and unable to get away, but was hoping to meet them soon. "Given the way I met Sorcha... That was a terrible shock," he said, patting a warm— yes, it was even brotherly—hand over hers. "I'm so sorry for that. I must have struck you as in-

credibly callous. I had heard a rumor my father
had children in Ireland, but as you can imagine,
it was never discussed. When Cesar pulled me
aside and told me…I wanted to speak to you then,
but he said it wasn't the time. He was so livid I
was glad to get away with my life. Honestly,"
he said with an earnest nod as Sorcha's sisters
giggled. "But I— Oh, hello. Speak of the devil."

Tom picked up his hand off Sorcha's.

"What? Oh!" Sorcha turned in her seat to see
her husband striding through the pub toward
them, hair damp and tousled by the weather,
cheeks lightly stubbled in that rugged way he
liked to wear his beard. He wore a rain-speckled
suit and his eyes had dark bruises under them.

Her heart soared in excited reaction.

He stopped at the far end of the table and Sorcha was aware of the entire establishment qui-
eting.

Speaking of livid, she thought as he looked at
her. Was he angry she hadn't come home? He was
acting like a bloody dictator, if that's why he was
here, but honestly, what was wrong with her that
she was so darned happy to see him even when
he looked so grim?

She wasn't mentally prepared to face him,
though. She had married him in a state of de-
lusion, believing she could somehow reach his
heart, but she didn't know how to resume their

marriage now that the reality of his locked heart had been shown to her so bluntly.

Enrique squawked and Cesar dragged his gaze from predatory fixation on her to soften as he looked at his son. He took the boy from his auntie's lap and gave him a little toss into the air, kissing his cheek, then winked one eye against the baby's happy tap of his open hands against his face.

"I'm excited to see you, too. But I need to talk to your mother. Angela, would you mind?" He handed Enrique to Sorcha's mum, who agreed to take custody of her grandson with the special adoring blink she reserved for Cesar.

Then he held out a hand in Sorcha's direction. And because he was that arrogant and she was that obedient, she got to her feet on his wordless command.

He said to Tom in a very ominous tone, "You know, of course, that nothing said at this table has any legal bearing?"

"I do know that," Tom said with a faint, dry smile. "Your wife said the exact same thing the moment I arrived."

Cesar looked at her. "I've always taken you for a soft touch."

"I can be cold-blooded and practical when necessary," she said, adding in a joke that fell flat, "I learned it from the best."

Cesar's eyes narrowed in a look he might give a mortal adversary. "I've booked us into the hotel. Call if he needs us," he said with a nod at Enrique and pulled her away without even her purse.

The hotel was down the block and across the street, just far enough to keep them from talking as they ran through the rain, trying not to get soaked. At the desk, the same woman who'd given Sorcha the dirty look last time lifted supercilious brows as Cesar told her he had a room reserved.

As he took the key, he said to the woman, "My father is Javiero Montero y Salazar, *el Excelentísimo* Señor Grandeza de España. I'm his eldest son. That means I and my wife will be the Duke and Duchess of Castellon one day. That sort of thing seems to impress your management, given that we're in the suite you reserve for royalty and you hang photos of titled guests on the wall." He pointed at the framed and signed snapshot of an actor who'd been knighted. "Your bad manners reflect on you, not us. Do I need to have this conversation with your employer?"

"No, sir," the woman said, eyes wide, voice mousy.

He didn't say another word, just tugged Sorcha up to their room.

As he pressed the door closed and threw the

key on the side table, she said, "Do I finally get to ask what you're doing here?"

She was shaking and hoped he put it down to shivers at wearing damp clothes.

"Where should I be? Sitting in our empty house, waiting for you?" He threw off his wet jacket and moved to fetch a pair of towels from the powder room, handing one to her. "I had the feeling you weren't planning on coming back for a while. Is that true?"

She opened her mouth, but wasn't sure what to say. "I wanted to be sure things with Tom were okay," she lied. "These are the first contracts and legal briefs Mum's ever read. I want to go over them with her so I know she understands what she's signing."

"And then you were going to come home?" Cesar persisted.

Home. Her heartstrings plucked. This village where her family lived had always been home. That house on the hill had been home and could be again.

But home was a villa in Spain. Her heart knew that.

"Sorcha—"

"Don't be angry with me!" she said, pressing her towel to her face, then opening it across her shoulders and hugging it around her wet shirt and over her damp hair. "I know you weren't raised with love. *To* love. I know it's a foreign concept to you, but I hoped, okay? I hoped for three years that you would fall in love with me and you didn't. In fact, you were going to marry someone else and I couldn't watch it. So I tried to leave and—"

"You've always loved me," he said, tossing his towel after his jacket and folding his arms. "Did you tell me that day? In Valencia?"

"Maybe," she mumbled. "I might have whispered it after we made love and I thought you were asleep."

He was looking at her like he always did when the topic of That Day came up. Like he wanted to drill inside her head and take possession of the memories she held just beyond his reach.

"And you haven't said anything all this time because…?"

"Because of this!" She waved between them. "If you had ever loved anyone, Cesar, you would know how painful this is. To love someone and feel like you can't have them is excruciating!" She threw the towel away and hugged herself, cold and miserable and feeling pitiful.

"Would it feel anything like waking in a hospital and knowing there was one person you wanted to see, only one person who could possibly ground you, one person who would act like they gave a serious damn about you almost dying, then hear that she had quit and left the country? Would it feel something like that, Sorcha?"

She eyed him. Was this a trick?

"Did you really feel like that?" she asked faintly. "Because I kept telling myself you'd call if..." She shrugged. "Diega chased me off, you know that."

"I didn't then. All I knew was that you were gone and I was so angry..." He shook his head as if just the memory of how incensed he had been still had the power to steal his speech.

"I'm sorry," she said sincerely. "I wanted to be there."

He shrugged, both acceptance and dismissal in the gesture. "I didn't think you would come because you loved me. I thought you would come because you're Sorcha."

She had to smile at that, thinking there was a compliment buried in there even though she wasn't sure exactly what it was.

"You're right about love being foreign to me. My parents are...the way they are. Mother came from a title without money. She had to marry well and bring her family back into the class she thought she belonged in. My father? Honestly, I suspect he's one of those genius savants who doesn't feel emotions like the average person. The one time I let myself grow fond of someone, to trust in friendship—not love, but friendship—

I was kicked in the face. Do you know when I finally began to understand what love looked like? What it was?"

She shook her head.

"The day your niece went missing. You were upset beyond anything I've ever witnessed. I get it now, of course. If Enrique somehow disappeared...I can't even say the words without my heart rate climbing. But that day I understood that you loved that little girl and I could see what it would cost you if she didn't turn up. It was not a good advertisement for love. It was a terrifying caution against it."

"But you love Enrique, don't you?" she asked anxiously. That much she needed to hear.

"So much." His breath left him and his shoulders slumped in a kind of bemused defeat. "I can't imagine if the baby swap had happened and we didn't have him. Or if it hadn't happened and I didn't know about him at all. I should have said this sooner, Sorcha, but thank you. Thank you for having my son and bringing him into my life. He is, well, Rico said it best the other day. Enrique is the most important thing I have ever made. Thank you for making him with me."

A rush of emotion filled her eyes and made her sniff. At the same time, she had to wonder, if he loved his son... What about her? Could he not love her *a little*?

"I feel that way about him, too," she began, voice tight. "And I can't deny him his father or his birthright, but I don't know what to do about us. I'll come back to Spain, I will, but I'm going to need time."

"Sorcha." He came forward to take her hands. His were warm and hers chilly. He frowned at her cool fingers and pressed her hands between his own. "I'll never know what I said to Diega or why I crashed, but I am convinced that I went to tell her I couldn't marry her. I think I realized that day that I loved you, too."

"You don't have to say that," she said in a husky voice. "I already said I'd come back."

"No." He squeezed her hands. "What I'm feeling right now? It isn't easy to articulate, but it's *right*. I woke up from that crash and I was angry. Angry that I couldn't remember, angry that you were gone. Angry that I was marrying a woman I didn't want. Then the London hospital called and a million feelings hit me. Confusion and shock and—"

"More anger," she said.

"Relief," he said after a shrug of acceptance. "That I didn't have to marry Diega. That I would see you again. Lust," he said wryly and adjusted his grip so he held each of her hands cradled in each of his, thumbs drawing circles in her palms. "I don't do well in any sort of weakened position, you know that. I won't let anyone take advantage of me and since my crash, I've had this giant vulnerability of lost time. But once you were back in my life I began to feel I was coming back onto an even keel. I didn't see how much you meant to me. I admit that. There's been a lot to adjust to. Fatherhood, for one."

She nodded, unable to argue with that.

"But when you said you loved me, I was happy, Sorcha. I haven't been happy since…" He narrowed his eyes. "Since before my mother started pushing me to formalize my engagement. Do you know why I worked such late hours when you were at the office with me? Because *you were at the office with me*. Now I want to be home. Because that's where you are. Actually, now you're in Ireland and guess where I am?"

She pressed her lips to keep them from trembling. His face was blurring and she sniffed. "You're not just saying that?"

"When have you ever known me to be sentimental for the sake of it? Sorcha, I *love* you."

She sniffed again and threw her arms around him. "I love you, too."

"Finally," he groaned, tightening his arms around her.

"I love you *so much*." She started to cry.

"No, *mi amor*," he murmured, catching her up

then sitting her in his lap as he lowered to the sofa. "Please don't cry."

"Happy tears," she assured him, arms around his neck. Kissing his throat. "Happy, happy, happy."

He cradled the side of her face and covered her mouth, kissing her sweetly. Lovingly. Then he looked into her eyes. "I'm happy, too. I didn't know love could feel like this. So beautiful. So right. I adore you, *mi amor*. Stay with me always."

"I will," she promised.

EPILOGUE

SORCHA DID WHAT she swore she would never do and pulled rank with Cesar's assistant, overriding concerns that Señor Montero was anxiously awaiting the completion of this report and sending her out for a long lunch.

Then she knocked on his office door and walked in without waiting for him to grant entry.

"I said I didn't want to be—" He looked up, recognized her, recognized what she was *wearing*, and sat back, expression speculative.

Sorcha couched a smile, pleased to have just knocked her husband speechless.

Smoothing her hands down the blue skirt that was just a teensy bit too short to wear in the office, she walked toward him, dropping her purse in the first chair she passed, pausing to shrug out of her short jacket and revealing the top that was going to burst its buttons despite the fact Enrique had weaned ages ago. Apparently these postpregnancy breasts were here to stay.

Licking her lips, she leaned both hands on his desktop and said, "Do you know what today is?"

Cesar slowly leaned forward, like a man who was about to negotiate, but his one hand shot out to cuff her wrist, pinning her in that position of leaning forward across his desk. Without a word, he lifted his other hand and flicked her buttons.

The taut fabric loosened as the opening gaped, revealing her lacy bra. Her nipples, raised with anticipation as she'd prepared for this meeting, visibly protruded against the fine silk cups.

He casually moved the dangling sapphire pendant out of the way, resting it behind her shoulder so the chain gave a little pull across her neck. Then he leisurely enjoyed the view.

"I believe it's Tuesday," he said in a voice that held a rasp she recognized. He was really turned on. "The ninth."

"It is exactly five years since my date of hire," she announced.

His gaze finally came up to hers. "Well, aren't you the efficient PA, coming to tell me that." He flattened his hand over hers, like he was gluing her palm to the desktop. "Do *not* move."

He rose and came around the desk to stand behind her.

She could imagine what he saw: her skirt about to burst its seams over a bottom that was almost but not entirely back to her prepregnancy figure.

Her shoes were far too high and sexy for a real day of work in the office, but perfect for seducing one's husband with a bit of role playing.

She playfully arched her back and cocked a hip to ensure he had the best possible view.

"I believe a raise of some kind is in order," he murmured, and slowly began to lift her skirt.

She closed her eyes, instantly seduced by the warmth of his hands sliding up the outsides of her thighs, taking the hem of her skirt up, up, up. Her stomach fluttered. Cool air washed across her thighs. A moan of excitement began growing in her throat.

"Did you lock the door?" he asked, pausing.

"I am an extremely efficient PA, sir. The door is locked and the girl has been sent for a long lunch. The phone is going to voice mail."

"I love you," he groaned, hands finishing the job then splaying hotly across her buttocks. "You're naked!"

"I took them off in the ladies' room down the hall."

"You *want* to kill me, don't you?"

They almost killed each other. Two hours later, they were sprawled in a tangled heap across the sofa where they'd first made love, naked, champagne open on the table, bodies lethargic with sexual satisfaction, when they heard a thump beyond the door.

"If my ears don't deceive me, that's the sound of a handbag going into the desk drawer," Sorcha murmured.

Cesar cursed and they both sat up to reluctantly begin gathering their clothes.

"Oh, um—" She shot him a sheepish grin as she wriggled her skirt up her hips. "I had another reason for coming into the city today."

He sent her a disgruntled frown. "This wasn't a special trip for me?"

"I've been planning this for ages," she assured him with a flirty peck on his mouth. "But I was able to get an appointment this morning on short notice so it was convenient to take it."

"Where?" He glanced down at her skirt and she could hear him wondering who else had seen her in it. It wasn't *that* racy. He was the only one who saw it as a sexual invitation.

"The doctor," she replied. "Remember that thing we talked about a month or so ago? About whether Enrique would like a little brother or sister?"

He froze in tying his tie. "Are you serious? And you let me ravage you on the desk? Sorcha!" he scolded, coming across to pull her in close. His hands slid over her as if searching for damage.

"I'm fine!" she assured him. "I liked it."

"Well, we're going to be more gentle from now on. *Dios*, really? A baby? Feel my heart."

She pressed her palm to his chest, laughing at the race of it. Her own had been dancing since she'd begun to suspect.

"I'm going to be with you every minute," he promised.

"I know," she said, believing it. Excited for what was to come.

He was with her. He even napped alongside her after the midnight birth, waking to fetch their son when he cried and bringing him to her to nurse.

"Ha!" he said as he turned on his phone, ready to advise the world of their blessed event. "Look what came in from the Ferrantes while we were in the delivery room."

He showed her a photo of a blissful Octavia holding their newborn daughter.

"Good thing we didn't meet them in London," Sorcha said.

Octavia had jokingly invited her to, once they'd shared their pregnancy news with each other.

"They might have mixed them up again. You could have wound up with a girl," Sorcha teased.

"I would love a girl," Cesar said, cupping a gentle hand behind his son's head. "I love my boys, but a girl would be nice sometime in the future." He kissed her. "If you're up to it."

"Do you hear yourself?"

"I do and I'm astonished. But unashamed. I love my family. Thank you, Sorcha. Thank you for breaking your promise not to have sex with me."

"My pleasure," she assured him.

*****

*If you haven't already, make sure you pick up
the first story in Dani Collins's fabulous duet*
THE WRONG HEIRS,
THE MARRIAGE HE MUST KEEP
Available now!

LARGER-PRINT BOOKS!
GET 2 FREE LARGER-PRINT NOVELS PLUS
2 FREE GIFTS!

HARLEQUIN

Romance

From the Heart, For the Heart

YES! Please send me 2 FREE LARGER-PRINT Harlequin® Romance novels and my 2 FREE gifts (gifts are worth about $10). After receiving them, if I don't wish to receive any more books, I can return the shipping statement marked "cancel." If I don't cancel, I will receive 4 brand-new novels every month and be billed just $5.09 per book in the U.S. or $5.49 per book in Canada. That's a savings of at least 15% off the cover price! It's quite a bargain! Shipping and handling is just 50¢ per book in the U.S. and 75¢ per book in Canada.* I understand that accepting the 2 free books and gifts places me under no obligation to buy anything. I can always return a shipment and cancel at any time. Even if I never buy another book, the two free books and gifts are mine to keep forever.

119/319 HDN GHWC

Name _____ (PLEASE PRINT) _____

Address _____ Apt. # _____

City _____ State/Prov. _____ Zip/Postal Code _____

Signature (if under 18, a parent or guardian must sign)

Mail to the **Reader Service:**
IN U.S.A.: P.O. Box 1867, Buffalo, NY 14240-1867
IN CANADA: P.O. Box 609, Fort Erie, Ontario L2A 5X3
Want to try two free books from another line?
Call 1-800-873-8635 or visit www.ReaderService.com.

* Terms and prices subject to change without notice. Prices do not include applicable taxes. Sales tax applicable in N.Y. Canadian residents will be charged applicable taxes. Offer not valid in Quebec. This offer is limited to one order per household. Not valid for current subscribers to Harlequin Romance Larger-Print books. All orders subject to credit approval. Credit or debit balances in a customer's account(s) may be offset by any other outstanding balance owed by or to the customer. Please allow 4 to 6 weeks for delivery. Offer available while quantities last.

Your Privacy—The Reader Service is committed to protecting your privacy. Our Privacy Policy is available online at www.ReaderService.com or upon request from the Reader Service.

We make a portion of our mailing list available to reputable third parties that offer products we believe may interest you. If you prefer that we not exchange your name with third parties, or if you wish to clarify or modify your communication preferences, please visit us at www.ReaderService.com/consumerchoice or write to us at Reader Service Preference Service, P.O. Box 9062, Buffalo, NY 14240-9062. Include your complete name and address.

HRLP15

LARGER-PRINT BOOKS!
GET 2 FREE LARGER-PRINT NOVELS PLUS
2 FREE GIFTS!

HARLEQUIN®

super romance®

More Story...More Romance

YES! Please send me 2 FREE LARGER-PRINT Harlequin® Superromance® novels and my 2 FREE gifts (gifts are worth about $10). After receiving them, if I don't wish to receive any more books, I can return the shipping statement marked "cancel." If I don't cancel, I will receive 4 brand-new novels every month and be billed just $5.94 per book in the U.S. or $6.24 per book in Canada. That's a savings of at least 12% off the cover price! It's quite a bargain! Shipping and handling is just 50¢ per book in the U.S. or 75¢ per book in Canada.* I understand that accepting the 2 free books and gifts places me under no obligation to buy anything. I can always return a shipment and cancel at any time. Even if I never buy another book, the two free books and gifts are mine to keep forever.

132/332 HDN GHVC

Name	(PLEASE PRINT)	

Address		Apt. #

City	State/Prov.	Zip/Postal Code

Signature (if under 18, a parent or guardian must sign)

Mail to the **Reader Service:**
IN U.S.A.: P.O. Box 1867, Buffalo, NY 14240-1867
IN CANADA: P.O. Box 609, Fort Erie, Ontario L2A 5X3

Want to try two free books from another line?
Call 1-800-873-8635 today or visit www.ReaderService.com.

* Terms and prices subject to change without notice. Prices do not include applicable taxes. Sales tax applicable in N.Y. Canadian residents will be charged applicable taxes. Offer not valid in Quebec. This offer is limited to one order per household. Not valid for current subscribers to Harlequin Superromance Larger-Print books. All orders subject to credit approval. Credit or debit balances in a customer's account(s) may be offset by any other outstanding balance owed by or to the customer. Please allow 4 to 6 weeks for delivery. Offer available while quantities last.

Your Privacy—The Reader Service is committed to protecting your privacy. Our Privacy Policy is available online at www.ReaderService.com or upon request from the Reader Service.

We make a portion of our mailing list available to reputable third parties that offer products we believe may interest you. If you prefer that we not exchange your name with third parties, or if you wish to clarify or modify your communication preferences, please visit us at www.ReaderService.com/consumerschoice or write to us at Reader Service Preference Service, P.O. Box 9062, Buffalo, NY 14240-9062. Include your complete name and address.

HSRLP15

LARGER-PRINT BOOKS!

GET 2 FREE LARGER-PRINT NOVELS PLUS 2 FREE GIFTS!

⊕HARLEQUIN®

I N T R I G U E

BREATHTAKING ROMANTIC SUSPENSE

YES! Please send me 2 FREE LARGER-PRINT Harlequin® Intrigue novels and my 2 FREE gifts (gifts are worth about $10). After receiving them, if I don't wish to receive any more books, I can return the shipping statement marked "cancel." If I don't cancel, I will receive 6 brand-new novels every month and be billed just $5.49 per book in the U.S. or $6.24 per book in Canada. That's a saving of at least 11% off the cover price! It's quite a bargain! Shipping and handling is just 50¢ per book in the U.S. and 75¢ per book in Canada.* I understand that accepting the 2 free books and gifts places me under no obligation to buy anything. I can always return a shipment and cancel at any time. Even if I never buy another book, the two free books and gifts are mine to keep forever.

199/399 HDN GHWN

Name _____ (PLEASE PRINT)

Address _____ Apt. #

City _____ State/Prov. _____ Zip/Postal Code

Signature (if under 18, a parent or guardian must sign)

Mail to the **Reader Service:**
IN U.S.A.: P.O. Box 1867, Buffalo, NY 14240-1867
IN CANADA: P.O. Box 609, Fort Erie, Ontario L2A 5X3

Are you a subscriber to Harlequin® Intrigue books and want to receive the larger-print edition?
Call 1-800-873-8635 today or visit www.ReaderService.com.

* Terms and prices subject to change without notice. Prices do not include applicable taxes. Sales tax applicable in N.Y. Canadian residents will be charged applicable taxes. Offer not valid in Quebec. This offer is limited to one order per household. Not valid for current subscribers to Harlequin Intrigue Larger-Print books. All orders subject to credit approval. Credit or debit balances in a customer's account(s) may be offset by any other outstanding balance owed by or to the customer. Please allow 4 to 6 weeks for delivery. Offer available while quantities last.

Your Privacy—The Reader Service is committed to protecting your privacy. Our Privacy Policy is available online at www.ReaderService.com or upon request from the Reader Service.

We make a portion of our mailing list available to reputable third parties that offer products we believe may interest you. If you prefer that we not exchange your name with third parties, or if you wish to clarify or modify your communication preferences, please visit us at www.ReaderService.com/consumerschoice or write to us at Reader Service Preference Service, P.O. Box 9062, Buffalo, NY 14240-9062. Include your complete name and address.

HILP15

YES! Please send me **The Montana Mavericks Collection** in Larger Print. This collection begins with 3 FREE books and 2 FREE gifts (gifts valued at approx. $20.00 retail) in the first shipment, along with the other first 4 books from the collection! If I do not cancel, I will receive 8 monthly shipments until I have the entire 51-book Montana Mavericks collection. I will receive 2 or 3 FREE books in each shipment and I will pay just $4.99 US/ $5.89 CDN for each of the other four books in each shipment, plus $2.99 for shipping and handling per shipment.*If I decide to keep the entire collection, I'll have paid for only 32 books, because 19 books are FREE! I understand that accepting the 3 free books and gifts places me under no obligation to buy anything. I can always return a shipment and cancel at any time. My free books and gifts are mine to keep no matter what I decide.

263 HCN 2404   463 HCN 2404

Name	(PLEASE PRINT)	
Address		Apt. #
City	State/Prov.	Zip/Postal Code

Signature (if under 18, a parent or guardian must sign)

Mail to the **Reader Service:**

IN U.S.A.: P.O. Box 1867, Buffalo, NY 14240-1867
IN CANADA: P.O. Box 609, Fort Erie, Ontario L2A 5X3

MMLPBPA15